The HUNDERSON ADVENTURES
The Adventure Begins

To whom it may concern,

We are writing to inform this party that one known as John Hunderson Sr. is dead. There was nothing we could do when we arrived. We are sorry that this is the way this party must find out.

The very best of wishes in further travels.

Signed,

S

THE HUNDERSON ADVENTURES
The Adventure Begins

A Novel

Michael T. Edwards

The Hunderson Adventures

Published by Wisdom House Books, Inc.
Chapel Hill, North Carolina 27516 USA
1.919.883.4669 | www.wisdomhousebooks.com

Wisdom House Books is committed to excellence in the publishing industry.
Book design copyright © 2022 by Wisdom House Books, Inc. All rights reserved.
Cover illustration by Anastasia Nesterova
Cover and Interior Design by Ted Ruybal
Published in the United States of America

Paperback ISBN: 978-1-7366582-0-8
LCCN: 2021923589

1. YAF001000 | YOUNG ADULT FICTION / Action & Adventure / General
2. FAM021000 | FAMILY & RELATIONSHIPS / Friendship
3. HUM015000 | HUMOR / Form / Anecdotes & Quotations

First Edition

25 24 23 22 21 20 / 10 9 8 7 6 5 4 3 2 1

Table of Contents

# Prologue

Within the world of Direfell, there are four ends, each spanning vast distances between each other: North, South, East, and West. Within each end are different regions and locations dedicated to its creators.

On the East End of Direfell there is the stone city of Wakesfield where many dwell and if one travels far enough south, they will discover an inn known as the Bulwark Bazaar. Travelling even farther south is where Focal Point Field resides. North of Wakesfield is Candlelit Castle and slightly to the west, the Twilight Region.

Travelling even farther west means going through the dark, encompassing Forest Region. On the other side, the West End Junkyard and West End River. The Whirlwind, and Ice Regions can be seen, provided one survives their journey through the Forest Region.

The Feared Five, first to have travelled Direfell, discovered the region's and location's secrets hidden deep within.

Of these five men, there was an achiever known as the Clayappose. He, although equal with the Feared Five, sought to be better than his companions. The Clayappose trained vigorously over the course of his life inventing new spells and fighting styles. Some say he's dead, others say he wanders the regions still, waiting for his heir to learn his most powerful spell.

 *Chapter 1*

On the East End of Direfell, there laid a massive city made entirely of stone: every building, every block, every possible passing. The city had its own quadrants: the Old Bomb Bunkers of the North, the Flower Beds of the East, the Water Wells of the South, and the Watchtowers of the West.

Wakesfield, or the Stone City, had interminable stone streets, accompanied by tall, black lampposts that illuminated the streets with their bright amber flames.

The vast history and lore of this city, as told by the city wanderers, included tales about the wishing wells or arguments about which building was the tallest in the city—the clock tower or the watchtower.

Despite the arguments, told among the city folk of Wakesfield, the clock tower was the tallest. Certainly taller than the Epoch Tower of Wakesfield, and far higher than any watchtower to the west, except one tower, far off in another land.

Much like this tower outside of Wakesfield, the story took place past the giant citadel-like walls, in the depths of a forest. It began in a simple stone building, on a simple, quiet stone street, where two boys lived: John "Johnny" Hunderson Jr. and Billy Hunderson. The Hunderson home was one of the last built in this old style, large and imposing. To the left of their building were other, giant, stone buildings that went high up into the sky. To the right of their building, homes and buildings favored the style that emerged after the last war. They were smaller, less complicated, and possessed flat roofs.

Johnny and Billy were quiet types; they always kept to themselves and never caused any trouble. They did what most residents of Wakesfield did, enduring the daily life before them and carrying out their business without sticking their noses in the business of others.

As another wave passed, Johnny was that much older and knowledgeable. His curiosity piqued more and more; his quest for understanding a simple question that burned in his mind burned harder and stronger. This led to Johnny sneaking out at night while his brother was asleep and returning in the morning just before he awoke.

He snuck out to gather as much information as he possibly could about this project. He needed answers. Johnny had ceaselessly worked on this project that had consumed his focus for the better part of his life. To fail would mean never uncovering the truth or having closure on the death of his father, John Hunderson Sr. A mild-mannered man such as Johnny had been driven to a madness of sorts—he needed to find out who killed his father, and why. He had become so consumed by this project; it had affected his life in ways he didn't even think it could. Johnny was enlisted in the Army Commando of the Protective Force, or A.C.P.F., much like his older brothers. However, when news of the death of his father reached Johnny, he abandoned this and returned home to be with his younger brother Billy.

Johnny knew that sneaking out was wrong and that he should include his brother Billy in his quest for answers, but to Johnny, Billy just wasn't up to his standards. Johnny was proficient in his fighting style; he studied fighting in the way of the Black Dragon, a fighting style created by his father. This was why Johnny did not consider Billy to be ready; to sit around and wait for Billy to finish his training wasted too much of the precious time they had to uncover the death of their father. On this particular night, Johnny did not stay out too late, and he returned back to his home and actually got some sleep for once.

As another night died, the next one rose like a phoenix from its ashes—the warmth of the sun kissed the windowpanes as it encroached through and it touched Johnny's face. His eyes slowly opened like a door being opened when having arrived home late at night. He rolled out of his bed and walked down the hall to his brother Billy's room and woke him.

"Billy, it's time to get up," said Johnny.

"Morning already, huh?"

"Yes, now let's get moving. We have a lot to do today."

"We're still going to Coheod Market, right."

"Of course. Now move it."

The two of them made their way to the inner city, which was a full day's travel. As the brothers walked, the giant clocktower constantly tapped its *tap tap tap*. The sound surrounded them like the different pitched voices of the inhabitants of Wakesfield; the clocktower's strum matched each step the Hunderson brothers took on the cobblestone streets.

"I wonder what the merchants will have out today," said Billy cheerfully.

"Hopefully, it's something new," Johnny responded.

With each step, the brothers got farther away from their home.

The sun slowly began to set, just as the brothers reached the outskirts of Coheod Market. When they arrived at the inner city. Johnny glanced down at a stand and reached for a red apple. He clasped it in his hands then tossed it up into the air and when the apple fell back down, he caught it perfectly on the back of his hand. He then tossed up the apple again and this time caught it with his teeth, then proceeded to take a bite.

"The apples are extremely juicy today, Billy!" exclaimed Johnny gleefully.

Billy looked toward Johnny and a smile appeared on his face.

The owner of the fruit stand grimaced at Johnny, his hands smoothed out the front of his ruffled merchant's vest as he watched the young man in front of him bite into the apple he had yet to pay for.

"That'll be two pelf, sir," said the merchant to Johnny.

Johnny reached into his pocket and pulled out a brown, slightly worn felt sack. Johnny pulled the gold string and opened up the sack. He pulled out two silver square coins and handed them to the merchant.

"For the apple."

"Thank you, sir," replied the merchant happily, his attitude improved after receiving payment for the apple.

"You ever wonder why we call it 'pelf' and not just simply money or coins?" asked Johnny to the merchant.

"I do not, sir," replied the merchant in a confused tone.

"Well, money is money, I suppose," said Johnny.

"Right you are, sir, have a lovely day!"

Johnny and Billy left the merchant's stand and continued walking on down the cobblestone street. With each step, the merchant got smaller and smaller before he soon disappeared into the distance. Johnny and Billy passed many shops and merchants on the main road, known as Coheod Market.

"Hey, Johnny?"

"Yes, Billy?"

"Speaking of why money is called pelf, why do you think the road where mostly all of the merchants are, is called Coheod Market?"

"That actually dates back a bit. I remember dad telling me about this. He told me a lot of interesting things that day...just a few bits before he left."

Johnny paused in his speech and continued walking on next to Billy, blank faced and empty.

"Johnny?"

Johnny gave no response.

"Johnny?!"

"Yes, sorry, Billy."

"Coheod Market."

"Yes, yes, I remember dad telling me that when Wakesfield was first constructed, the inhabitants and builders wanted a common area for people to go. Merchants would set up their stands, then markets became more popular, followed by buildings selling items for travel or food, and before you know it, Coheod Market was born!"

"That's great and all, but it still doesn't really explain why it has its name."

"I suppose that it's named Coheod Market due to how closely it sounds to the word coed—people are all able to mingle and converse here. Enough about the market, we must press on to our destination,"

Johnny said firmly.

"Where exactly are we going?" asked Billy.

"Some place we haven't been in quite some time."

"That's so incredibly vague. Will you please for once stop treating me like I can't understand something? I'm more than capable."

"Said the guy who just asked me about the meaning of Coheod Market."

They both laughed and continued walking on bantering back and forth, as siblings often do.

"Will you at least tell me when we're close, Johnny?"

"Close to getting smacked or to our destination?" asked Johnny, sarcastically, "I swear you're too inquisitive sometimes and it's starting to annoy."

"If you told me, I wouldn't have to keep asking," said Billy.

Johnny scoffed.

"Please don't deal in absolutes with me, thank you kindly."

"'Thank you kindly' . . . Sometimes I wish we'd speak like actual brothers and not this proper language, ya know?"

"Yeah I get you, Billy but a proper conversation leads to a proper focus."

Johnny and Billy walked farther and farther from Coheod Market, which made up a major part of Wakesfield's inner city. The brothers were used to travelling long distances on foot without much rest.

"Johnny, we got some supplies from the market first thing this morning and we're still walking."

"What's your point, Billy?"

"Well, soon it's going to get dark," said Billy.

"Wakesfield is lit up with so many lampposts, it's blinding. I'd rather it be day; it's almost too bright at nighttime you can't even tell it's dark at all."

As the brothers walked, the sun began to set, and the lampposts Johnny had just mentioned began to get ignited. The flames that are used to light the lampposts burn long into the night so there wasn't any worry about having to reignite one during the night.

Johnny and Billy exited fully from the cobblestone street and stepped onto a brown, dirt path. As Johnny and Billy stepped onto the dirt path, some dust kicked up. With each step the dirt beneath them got on their brown high-top boots, extending up to right beneath their kneecaps. Johnny put up the hood on his brown poncho as his black hair swirled around. Billy tripped over himself as they continued walking on the dirt path.

"Walk much?" asked Johnny with a chuckling tone.

"Sorry, it's getting harder to see now."

"That's because the lampposts don't extend out to this part of the city. They seem interminable everywhere else, except for any part of the city that isn't cobblestone."

"We have our lanterns we can always use."

"I'd rather not draw any attention to our whereabouts right now, Billy."

"Why?"

"Just don't use your lantern, all right? I'll explain everything once we reach our destination."

Johnny and Billy continued down the dirt path until they encountered a few scarce trees—miniature in size as compared to those in a forest. They had a light brown bark and their leaves were slowly falling and transforming from green to a dark brown.

"Why do these trees vary in size?" asked Billy.

"The trees were all planted probably thirty waves ago, well before our time. Dad said they only grow one foot ever two halves."

"Two halves? Why not just say a wave? It's the same thing."

"It's almost the same thing," said Johnny in a condescending tone.

"You're trying to tell me that two halves aren't one wave? Next you'll tell me that one quarter isn't one quarter of a wave."

"The terms created for time are used loosely, Billy, but the most accurate measurement of time we use is waves. You're fifteen waves while I'm seventeen. It's a lot more accurate than saying I'm seventeen waves and two halves."

"Why? You are halfway to having another wave pass and turning eighteen."

"I don't know, Billy, that's like the best explanation I've got. Okay? It's not a big deal, as long as you know time is passing, does its accuracy really matter?"

Although there were slight variations, most of the trees were about fifteen feet tall. They were planted to provide solar energy to the city. The townspeople found this plan ridiculous, so it was abandoned and the trees were left unattended. They were left in disrepair, able to grow messy and unkempt. As a result, this part of the city didn't match the general tidiness of Wakesfield. The path was dirt instead of cobblestone, the trees weren't neatly trimmed and primed like those in Coheod Market. Overgrown grass teemed with a dead, brown color and blended in so well with the dirt path, it could hardly be told if there was even grass there.

"We shall spend the night here, Billy, what do you say?" asked Johnny.

"That's fine with me. We haven't spent the night here since—"

Billy stops mid-sentence and squints his eyes in attempts to get a better view, then continued speaking, this time with a new thought.

"A messenger? We must have a parcel!"

"How did he find us?" asked Johnny.

Johnny turned around and faced the same way Billy was and they both saw a man dressed in short baby blue shorts, brown sandals, wrapped up and strapped around his lower leg, up to his calves. This man was also wearing a grayish-silver tunic and a giant, four-foot brown, leather backpack. The messenger's backpack extended well above the height of his head, indicating that it was full of items for others, ranging from letters, parcels, and other lore.

"My deepest apologies for interrupting, but this here is for you."

The messenger took off his giant backpack, set it down on the ground, and a puff of dust rose as he did. He dug around for a moment. He pulled out a white enveloped letter, rolled up like a scroll, and presented it to Johnny. Johnny took the letter from the messenger and gave him a nasty glare.

"How did you find us?" asked Johnny.

"Us messengers not only give information but also gather it."

Both Johnny and Billy stared blankly at the messenger.

"I asked around, sir."

"Anything else?" asked Johnny, in a nasty tone.

"Nothing more, sir."

"Off you go then," said Johnny.

"Very well, sir. Best of luck with your travels or whatever it is you two are doing out here."

Travels?" questioned Johnny.

"It's an expression us messengers say, sir. Seeing as we spend our days travelling all over, delivering items."

"Ah. Very well," remarked Johnny.

The messenger closed the flap on his bag and swung it back over his shoulders. There was a soft thud as the bag made contact with the messenger's back.

Johnny watched as the messenger took his leave before he took the letter and untied it. He did this by pulling on the one end of the crimson ribbon which kept the letter wrapped up in its scroll like form. Johnny's eyes scanned the letter and once he finished reading it, he clenched it in his fist.

"What does it say?" asked Billy, eagerly.

"Nothing I haven't told you before. In fact, it's one of the same. Whoever sent this letter knows who we are, as you only send out two copies of the same letter if you know your party is alive."

"You think it'd be the other way around. If you know they're alive then you'd only send one, right?" asked Billy.

"You would think, but instead they send out two to ensure that the intended party receives the letter," replied Johnny, "Anyway, get some rest. I'll tell you what, tomorrow we'll go on an adventure. We'll go do something new and exciting!"

"We haven't been on an adventure in a long time! I can't even fully recall our last adventure," stated Billy, excitedly.

"It was probably the one where we went out with dad on the scouting trip."

"Oh yeah! And you—"

"Yes, I had to fight some concrete falcon."

"That thing was like a statue!" exclaimed Billy.

"Not like any statue I'd ever seen," Johnny said with a cheerful tone. Johnny looked at Billy.

"Everything okay, Johnny?" asked Billy.

A smile appeared on Johnny's face as he recalled the scouting trip.

"Get some rest, Billy."

Billy smiled before lying down to rest for the night. Johnny watched as Billy got adjusted. It was true that the information on the letter wasn't anything new. In fact, Johnny had received this exact same letter when he was enlisting in the A.C.P.F. Johnny finished up his entrance examination—the final step before being deployed. This meant that had Johnny continued on, he wouldn't have received this letter, as anything sent to a member of the A.C.P.F. is cataloged and kept in a secure file for the receiver until they return. If they do not return by means of death or abandonment, the file is given to the next of kin, be it an offspring or relative.

Johnny took his eyes off Billy and slinked toward a nearby tree. He sat down and leaned up against the tree, as the moonlight peeked through the trees and shined on him. Johnny turned to Billy and he waited a few moments to ensure Billy was sound asleep. Johnny slowly turned his head away from Billy and peered down at the lake—he rose from the tree and moved closer to the lake. He stood tall before the lake and he unclenched his fist and removed the letter to allow him to unfold it from its wrinkled state. It made a crinkling noise as Johnny unfolded the letter; it was on a simple piece of parchment with no special raises or grooves, as most letters that messengers carry often were. When Johnny finally fully unfolded the letter, he read it.

> To whom it may concern,
> We are writing to inform this party that one known as John Hunderson Sr. is dead. There was nothing we could do when we arrived. We are sorry that this is the way this party must find out.
> The very best of wishes in further travels.
> Signed,
> S

Johnny stared down at the letter with a look of disdain. He then took the letter and crumpled it back up in his hands before he tossed it down into the lake. As he looked down at the letter that slowly shifted across the lake, he noticed some sap on his shirt from the tree against which he was leaning. He took off his shirt, dipped it into the lake and just stared at his reflection. He pulled the shirt out from the lake, wringed it, then tossed it over his shoulder and stood up straight.

He stared at his reflection in the lake, then paused and assessed his features. His blue eyes gazed back at him while a gentle breeze swirled through his long black hair. He realized that he had put too much time into this project, and he hadn't had time to cut it. Johnny took pride in all the work he'd put into his body.

Johnny pulled out a red bandana from his pocket and held it in his hand for a moment. He then lifted the bandana, tied it around his head, and peered down at his defined body. A faint smile overtook his pale complexion before it fell away into a scowl. He glared back down at the lake and focused his attention to his right upper chest where his Black Dragon's foot tattoo rested.

I've dedicated my time into the way of the Black Dragon, a fighting style aged back to the time of my father, a fighting style he invented and taught me. Not a day goes by where I don't think about him, where I don't stop my search.

Johnny ran his fingers over his tattoo and reflected on when he acquired it. Johnny closed his eyes for a moment and relived the memory.

# Chapter 2

A hand reached out and touched Johnny's shoulder. Johnny looked back and smiled at the sight of the person who had placed their hand on his shoulder.

"Are you ready, son?"

"Yes, father!"

"Good. Today is the day, Johnny, today is the day you become a man. You're going to be getting your Black Dragon's foot tattoo."

Johnny's smile widened as he looked up at his father—this ceremony of receiving the tattoo was held when a Hunderson became proficient in their style of fighting. All families had their own rituals and ceremonies to signify their offspring advancing to the next stage of their life.

"You're about the same age I was when I got my tattoo, Johnny."

"Really, dad?"

"Yes. I was at ten waves when I received mine and you're approaching your thirteenth wave. I'm very proud of you, Johnny."

"Thank you, dad!"

"I only wish your brothers could be here to see this monumental moment."

"As do I, but they're doing what's right; they're serving in the military."

"Not just any military, Johnny. The A.C.P.F."

"A.C.P.F.? What's that?"

"The Army Commando of the Protective Force. Direfell's finest military force."

"Wow, Direfell's finest, huh?" asked Johnny.

"That will be you someday, Johnny. You're still going to enlist, aren't you?"

"Of course! There's nothing I want more than to make you proud; I want to follow in your footsteps and do something great for Direfell."

John paused for a moment before he knelt down next to Johnny.

"You know, Johnny, I didn't actually enlist."

"You didn't? But I thought—"

"No, I was going to, but I . . ."

"What happened?" asked Johnny.

John paused.

"This was when I created the way of the Black Dragon, a style of fighting which many people use today."

"Right, I remember your telling me that!"

"However, one thing separates you from them," said John.

"What's that?"

"Close your eyes, Johnny, and let me tell you."

Johnny closed his eyes and as he did, his father John placed his palm on his upper right chest and pressed, hard. He held his hand there for a moment and when he released his hand, there was now the tattoo of the Black Dragon's foot.

"Open your eyes, son."

Johnny opened his eyes and looked down at his chest, a smile took over his whole face.

"Look into the water to get a better view of your reflection and see the Black Dragon's foot tattoo in all of its glory. Remember, this tattoo does not reflect your completion of your training, but instead the final level before mastery."

Johnny moved toward the lake and looked down at his body.

"How did you do that, Dad? Just by pressing your palm against my chest?"

"It's all about focusing your energy. It's kind of complicated to explain, but it's essentially like being branded. Only those who reached your same level will be able to do it."

"So, I could give the tattoo to Billy?"

"Yes, but only when he's ready."

"What about you?" asked Johnny.

"Me?"

"Yes, Dad."

"In the event I'm not there, perform the task, Johnny."

Johnny nodded.

"I have one more thing for you, Johnny."

John approached Johnny and pulled out a red bandana from his pocket. He tied it around Johnny's head.

"There. Now you have not only the tattoo, but the same bandana I had when I went out on my adventures."

"This is amazing!" said Johnny.

"I would like for you to read them someday, Johnny. Sure, I can recount them to you, but showing is better than telling, and there's no better way to do that than reading."

"Thank you for this, dad!"

"You earned it, Johnny. However, remember, your adventure doesn't stop here. Life will always test you and you must be ready for whatever life throws your way and never stray from the path you choose. Never lose control of yourself, who you are, or your focus, for once you do that you start to lose control of your path. Should you ever forget who you are, Johnny, return to the lake and reflect upon yourself."

Johnny stared silently at his father.

"Now come on! Let's get back home so you can tell Billy all about your new tattoo. Soon it'll be his turn to come down to the lake and get his tattoo!"

As John and Johnny made their way back toward their home, John took out a rock from his pocket and handed it to Johnny.

"Here, you may be the last person to ever touch this rock. Go ahead and toss it in the lake as a statement of this moment here."

Johnny complied and tossed the rock into the lake, as he did, the water began to shimmer and shake. As the lake returned to a calm nature, so too did Johnny. He opened his eyes and stared back down at the lake.

I can't believe it's been five waves since I came here with my father.

Johnny paused to reflect for a moment, then turned his head and glanced back at Billy. A cold breeze flowed through Johnny's hair. He adjusted his hair then looked at the path that led back to his house, then once more back at Billy.

Billy. Not William, not Bill, not Will, or Willy . . . My parents could have named him William Hunderson and have just called him Billy as a nickname, instead they chose to call him Billy. Yet here I stand as a junior to my father—he could have named any of my other siblings after him, but instead he chose me.

Johnny knelt and placed his hand in the lake and began swirling it around in the water.

It's as if he destined me to follow in his footsteps but I was never even given the chance to fulfill his own invention: the way of the Black Dragon. While I am quite proficient in this, I'm not perfect in it like my father and I'm beginning to wonder that, now since he's gone, if I'll ever complete my training.

Johnny took his hand out of the lake, shook off the excess water and looked back at Billy.

That stupid way of the Lion—a fighting style invented as a method of simply dodging attacks. While Billy had less time with our father than the rest of my siblings—the least, to be matter of fact—he still should be proficient in his fighting style. He's not.

Johnny's eyes travelled from Billy's body to the tree under which he slept. Johnny scanned the tree from bottom to top and took in every detail.

A tree has its own will to live and many think that watering it and nurturing it will help it grow, when in actuality, it is the tree's will to grow that makes it grow. A tree will grow up on its own and will become strong on its own, regardless of those there to nurture it.

Johnny went back to the tree before moving toward the lake. He sat down and rested his head against the tree and closed his eyes. Johnny was on the cusp of falling asleep as his body leaned more and more toward the ground, before eventually he fell over and hit the ground. This woke Johnny up. He slowly opened his eyes and he peered out to the trees. Johnny threw his head back and he rolled his eyes before he slowly rose to his feet. He pulled out a piece of parchment and wrote a note on it and left it next to Billy's body.

As the sun began to break past the trees, Johnny headed toward the path that led back to his house—a dirt brown path led out of the small, enclosed forest area, with its parsley green trees by the lake, and back onto the cobblestone streets of the main drag. This cobblestone street stretched on for quite some time and was the largest, most travelled upon street in all of Wakesfield.

As Johnny reached the main drag of Coheod Market, it is well into late afternoon. Johnny got some food from one of the merchants.

"Ah, Mr. Hunderson, always a pleasure to see you," said the cabbage merchant.

"Likewise. Listen, I've been looking around this area for that, you know, a certain person, and I haven't seen anyone suspicious. Keep an eye out, will ya?"

"Sure thing, Mr. Hunderson. Have you checked elsewhere?"

"That's what Billy and I will be doing tomorrow," said Johnny.

"Are you not returning to him tonight?"

"No. I have more to accomplish today, and I figured it'd be best if he weren't around to constantly pester me with his questions."

"Where will you check next?"

Johnny gave the merchant a blank stare.

"Very well, minding my place; tell, don't ask. I'll be sure to keep an eye out for any suspicious characters."

"Thank you."

Johnny reached into his brown pouch and handed the merchant some pelf. He then continued down the road.

As he proceeded down the road, he stopped at more shops, talking with more of the town's merchants.

"You there!" shouted the game merchant to Johnny.

"Yes?"

"Come here, boy, and test your luck!"

"Test my luck? You're testing yours right now by asking me to gamble," replied Johnny.

"Very well, young lad, carry on! . . . like you could win anyway with that attitude."

Johnny continued down Coheod Market's road, with each step he got closer to his home. Every possible space of this street there were merchants and people that crowded up the streets, constantly moving and shifting around. Despite all the people, not once did any of them ever bump into each other—their constant motion created a flow like a river's stream that overcame any debris or pebbles in its trajectory. Johnny looked down the streets he's passing whenever he can seize the chance; usually one must stick to looking strictly forward or risk bumping into someone, which might cause a fight . . . the last thing any person wants due to the city's police force.

Johnny glanced down one street which is totally dark, despite it being mid-morning. This street intrigued him so as he watched people walk down it and become whelmed in shadow. As he looked forward he found himself bumping into someone he does not expect. Thomas Bulwark—of the same family that owned and operated Bulwark Bazaar. He had known the Hunderson family for many waves as both of the families go back to the time of old.

"'Ello, Mr. Hunderson, steady on. You're up quite early."

"That would depend on one's term of 'early' seeing as it's mid-morning."

"Regardless, you're up and here you are."

"Yes, Thomas, here I am."

"Not too attentive today are we boy?"

"I always am," Johnny said in a firm tone.

"Not so much today. Something have your attention?"

"Yes, and it wonders as to why we're still conversing in the middle of the street. Might we take this conversation elsewhere?" asked Johnny, sarcastically.

"Elsewhere like your mind?" asked Thomas.

Johnny gave Thomas a look before both he and Thomas moved off to the side where it's less travelled.

"It's that street that I passed."

"The one in a looming shadow?"

"Yes," replied Johnny, "And I wonder for how long it has existed."

"Quite some time, but that street is a conversation for another day," Thomas said with a smirk.

"What do you mean?" asked Johnny.

Thomas looked at Johnny more sternly.

"You're going on an adventure, aren't you?"

"What makes you say that?"

"Intuition."

Johnny rolled his eyes.

"Or the very fact that I've been around these parts for a long time now, Johnny, and I too have known your family for a long time. Every time one of you Hunderson boys is off to go do something you always stop down at the lake."

"That doesn't mean that—it's just something we do, a tradition of sorts. Now it's Billy's time."

"Ah yes, pardon me, I didn't mean to pry."

"People that don't mean to pry don't feel the need to say they didn't mean to pry," Johnny said with a grimace.

"Very well. I do hope you find what you're looking for. Oh, and one more thing," Thomas said leaning in closer to Johnny, "You might want to consider stepping outside the city for this adventure."

Johnny's eyes went dead when Thomas finished his statement. *Outside the city?* he wondered.

Johnny came to and pulled back from Thomas.

"Or am I prying again?" Thomas said with a chuckle.

"Until next time, Thomas!"

"Yes, next time."

Johnny nodded.

"The adventure begins," said Thomas.

Johnny gave a faint smile to Thomas and replied, "I suppose an adventure is about to begin."

"No matter where in the world you go, Johnny, always remember: Don't let the world move around you. You move around the world."

Johnny nodded and continued on his way back to his house, leaving both Thomas and the shadowy street in the distance. Johnny slowly maneuvered his way back into the crowded street until he finally reached the cross section. The cross section is the center most part of the Stone City; there are four large streets that intersected, the largest of which, Johnny stood on. As he continued walking, nighttime approached and the sun began to set, meaning the bright lampposts will soon be lit. This, too, means the city's police force patrols will have doubled.

Chapter 3

Having finally reached his home, Johnny paused for a moment. The house was made entirely up of stone and was not the largest, nor the smallest, home on the street. The stones had archaic details engraved into them, tiny notches that were a blend of a lighter and darker grays. These marked the house as the last of this style, a terminating point in the city. Everything past the Hunderson home was built in the newer, post-war style.

In front of the home, there was a tiny flower bed out front with a multitude of different colored flowers planted in the soft soil. As Johnny approached the front door, he jiggled the handle.

All this time and this handle is just impossible to fix.

Johnny pressed his shoulder against the front of the door and, while he jiggled the handle, shoved his shoulder into the front door, opening it.

I suppose we are lucky the door does get stuck, seeing as our lock is broken. If not for that, we might get robbed like the older folks in the northern part of the city.

This house was once home to many. Many of whom are now off on their own adventures or have sadly moved on from this world. The house of Hunderson is known to most of the city locals. The Hunderson family is a fantastic family, many of whom have served and fought in the wars that have plagued this land. He glanced it over once, then opened the door. Johnny pushed the door open slowly and it creaked as it swung open wide.

In no way are we noble, yet people seem to know us from all over. It's crazy to think how much weight our family name carries.

He then made for the stairs and put his hand on the wooden banister and ascended the steps, slowly, gliding his hand up the banister with each step he took. Johnny headed for his room and as he did, he passed vacant rooms in the house. On the door of these vacant rooms there were the names of his siblings. The first name was Derex, the oldest offspring of John Hunderson Sr.

Derex, I do wish you well. I haven't seen you in so many waves, but I do hope you're doing well. I can't even remember your face anymore.

Derex had lived in this world for twenty-five waves, making the age gap between both he and Johnny just enough where he was around when Johnny was younger, but not long enough to see him grow up and receive his Black Dragon's foot tattoo.

I wonder how different things would be if you, like me, didn't enlist. Would you be around to help me avenge our father?

Derex was the first to enlist in the ongoing war and spent the most time with his father and mother. He was very strong and intelligent—he picked up the way of the Black Dragon quickly from his father's teachings. The last thing Johnny had heard about Derex is that he was a General in the A.C.P.F., a military group that protects the land from incoming forces and entities who try to plague the land.

The A.C.P.F. had been around for many waves—much of the Hunderson family had enlisted to fight in the war, as had other native families. Johnny continued along the wooden floor, with each step the floor creaked as his boots made their impact.

Hunter. Alex. I just can't believe you two are out there without me, serving. The timing of things was almost too perfect. If I hadn't received that letter when I did, Billy would've received it and, well, he wouldn't have been able to handle this on his own.

Next to Derex's room was a large room with two empty beds, with the names Hunter and Alex on the door. Alex was twenty-two, a full wave older than Hunter, and because of this, Alex waited until Hunter was of age to enlist and fight in the war. The last Johnny had heard about Hunter and Alex was that they were Commanders in the A.C.P.F.

He continued through the house and came across the next room. He ran his fingers across the name, then wiped some soot from his fingers onto his pants.

Then there's you. I still can't believe you ran away when you did. I also can't believe dad burned your name off the door. You were the closest to my age yet the furthest away from me.

The name on the door once read 'Ryan'—while he had been in this world for nineteen waves and closest to Johnny's age, he wasn't around enough due to his running away. Billy was also close to Johnny's age at fifteen waves, while Johnny was at seventeen. However, due to the birthdays, technically Ryan and Johnny are closer in age than Johnny and Billy.

Parents never seem to consider the toll the age difference between siblings will have as they get older. Sure, eight seems like a small number, but the difference between ten waves and eighteen waves means the difference between enlisting or not. Although the age to enlist is sixteen.

Johnny arrived at his room and entered it. Upon entering, he grabbed another backpack. He opened it up and took out some supplies and gear from his drawers and under his bed. He filled his backpack with a grappling hook, some food, and some water. As he made his way for the door he stopped and looked back surveying his room. He then moved on down, continuing to his parent's room. Johnny entered the room, slowly, then stopped and paused for a moment. He brushed off some dust and cobwebs from his body.

He hadn't been in this room since his parents were last here. Johnny then made his way over to a table next to the bed. He picked up the scrolls and pieces of parchment and blew off the dust from them. He set them down on the bed and combed through all of them, while he read them all and glanced at them.

The first piece of parchment Johnny saw was a map of Wakesfield that detailed the whole city. There were scribbles of writing across corners of the map, circling certain areas and listing items. From the main streets on Coheod Market, there were also smaller connecting streets interweaving these five main streets. One in particular was the shadowy street he passed earlier. The street had a thick, black line through it.

The street that was in front of Johnny when he was there earlier today led to the north—a place where the older citizens of Wakesfield resided. The north was also home to the Old Bomb Bunkers, a place of refuge during one of the wars. To Johnny's right was the path leading to the east, and nothing much is out there besides the Flower Beds, and their subsequent graveyard. Although, one point of interest was there and that is the clock tower. This clock tower was so large that it could be seen from very far off.

I can't believe how much more there is to Wakesfield. I have a lot more ground to cover if I'm going to get answers.

Some said that if the clock tower were to be scaled to its fullest height, that there was a whole other level of sky up there—a region of its own. Many stories and rumors are made up about the clock tower and they're all as true as their former. Possibly the most popular story told about the clock tower was the appearance of two men fighting atop of it, appearing as silhouettes against the moon's bright gleam.

On the opposite of Wakesfield, and to Johnny's left, sat the Watch-towers of the West. These towers were slightly shorter than the clock tower and are large in nature to be used to keep a watchful eye over Wakesfield. They were patrolled and operated by Wakesfield's police force and are off-limits to civilians.

Those are the last people I want to have an encounter with. If they're to ever stop me and recognize me in collusion with heckling merchants for answers, they'll surely arrest me right there. That'll sure put an end to my adventure.

Johnny lowered his eyes to the lower half of the map and looked over the written notes, barely legible as they were. To the south and leading away behind the Coheod Market street, lie the Waterwells: a series of wells where the many travelled to and into which they threw pelf in hopes of their wishes coming true. Yet another area of Wakesfield where the rumors fill the area just as much as the water fills the wells. One local claimed so much belief that one of the wells in particular didn't have water in it, instead it was an illusion projected by the other wells.

This local claimed to have even descended to the bottom of the well and travel to a different part of Direfell to a giant field, far off from Wakesfield. Much like the stories about the clock tower, they cannot be verified for anyone can make anything seem true if said convincingly enough times.

Wow. I wonder if these stories are true. How much else of Direfell can there possibly be?

Johnny pulled out another piece of parchment, blew off the dust, then ran his fingers across the top getting off any tiny specks of dust. The piece Johnny held in his hand was an extremely detailed map of Direfell. Johnny looked up from the map for a moment.

I wish I would have come in here sooner; I could have begun committing these maps to memory, or at least transcribed them into more legible writing.

Johnny looked back down at the map, his eyes danced all around it, looking at every possible area, region, and piece of writing.

The only issue with these parchments are the validity to them. Sure, dad told me he went on his travels, but I wonder if those stories were true or not.

Johnny started at the top of the map and began reading the scribbled notes.

I remember the names of a lot of these places from dad's stories. This map must be accurate. This explains why dad was off a lot, this is what he was doing! Exploring all of Direfell!

Johnny began reading the notes at the top of the map, those he could make out, of course.

I can't even make out the names of these outer regions . . . Evening List? Evermist? My father's writing is so archaic. And this one, down here . . . Right above Wakesfield. 'If it's knowledge to keep you merry, come to the library.' A riddle?

Johnny combed the entire map with his eyes. He turned and sat down on the bed and coughed when he did as his clothes went from black to a dusty gray for a second. Johnny quickly stood back up and dusted himself off. The bed, when ruffled, shot up dust.

Okay, bad idea sitting there.

Johnny sifted through more of the parchment, making sure to stuff the maps in his backpack. He picked up what appeared to be a book and opened it.

Finally!

Johnny held in his hands a tattered book, with torn pages and smudged writing.

Its handwritten title read *The Journal of John Hunderson*.

Johnny read through his father's journal and tried to understand it.

This is mostly gibberish. I suppose I can't blame dad as he did tell me I should read his journal someday, what I could decipher anyway.

Johnny flipped through a couple of pages and stopped when he came to one that had some color to it.

Hmm, some of these colors are crossed out while others are circled. Black is crossed out while orange is circled. Red has a giant 'x' over it. What do these colors mean?

Johnny flipped to the next page and read.

The Enchanted Eye Entities? What is this?

Johnny closely read this page.

Colored eyes and beasts and kings . . . this all seems so arbitrary. If only I could make out the rest of the writing on here. Was my father hunting beasts? We did go on scouting trips . . .

Johnny paused his reading for a moment and looked out the window.

Where did the time go?

Johnny closed his father's journal and placed it back on top of the table next to the bed.

In the wake of my being incapacitated, I wouldn't want this to fall into the wrong hands.

Johnny flipped through one more page and immediately pulled the journal closer to his face.

The ritual! I can read this and perform the tattoo ritual with Billy!

The other pieces of parchment all seemed to be random, and he couldn't make them out. They almost looked like a collection of files on people, but it was hard to tell due to the writing.

If I could just make out his writing, this would be a lot easier. What is that? East Wing? A building? A Wing, E Wing. I just can't tell!

Johnny picked up the rest of the parchment and in a tiff, lightly slammed them down on the table and then exited his parent's room, shutting the door behind him. He made his way down the corridor to a room marked Johnny. He set down his backpack, then got into bed.

Billy isn't going to believe this map! He loves maps. Maybe he can decipher it all.

Johnny closed his eyes and rested for the night, while back down at the lake, Billy also got ready for another night of sleep. He put out the small fire he had made to cook his food. He remembered Johnny's words of not wanting to draw attention. Billy went back to the tree under which he had slept last night. He read over the note Johnny left for him once more before he laid down and shut his eyes for the night.

After a restful night for both of the Hunderson brothers, another morning arrived. Johnny woke up from his bed, gathered his things, and headed out from his room. He headed to the stairs and placed his hand on the wooden banister once more. He exhaled then slowly descended the stairs. He reached the door, and gave it a hard pull open, then turned around and took one final look at his home before he closed the door.

Of course, why would I expect anything different?

Johnny had trouble shutting the door as the handle was stuck in the position it would be if the door were closed. Johnny attempted to wiggle the door. He was eventually successful in closing the door, and with his backpack over his shoulder, he made his way back to Billy. As he did this, he heard an unfamiliar voice.

"Hey! You there! Stop!"

Johnny came to a complete halt and turned to face the beckoning voice.

Chapter 4

Johnny turned and saw not one, but *three* members of the police.

"And just what do you think you're doing, robbing this house?"

"Excuse me?" questioned Johnny, "I happen—"

"Happen to be robbing this house. You're coming with me."

"Ease up, buddy. I live here. I'm a Hunderson."

Then two more members arrived.

"What is the problem here, Corporal?" asked a superior.

"I just saw this man leaving this house with not one, but two backpacks stuffed to the brim!"

"Has it entered your mind that this man lives here and is merely packing up gear?" asked the superior.

"Well, no, sir, it hasn't—"

"And has it crossed your mind that you're now hindering this man from his proceedings?"

"Sir, if I may—"

"You may not, Corporal."

"Yes, sir."

The man in charge approached Johnny.

"My apologies, sir. This man here is new and is still learning his place."

"Not to worry, Sergeant."

"You know your ranks well, young man."

"I have family members who are fighting in the war."

"Ah, yes, your older brothers. I remember them well."

"You do?" asked Johnny.

"Yes. I was very close with Hunter and Alex."

Johnny paused for a moment and wondered if this man knew or recognized him.

"Wallace?"

"You do remember your cousin," said Wallace.

"Wallace, yeah. Wow, I haven't seen you in quite some time. Didn't recognize you with those protective eye covers."

"Yes, it has been quite a long while, Johnny."

The two stared at one another as if they were both thinking about which memory to share next.

"I didn't think you'd still be around these parts. Not joining the war like your family?"

"Well, I— No. If I were going to do it, last quarter would have been the time to do it."

"Enlisting at the age of entry is a rare thing; many wait two waves until they're eighteen to enlist." Wallace paused for a moment, then continued, "Then again, you Hunderson boys have always been quick to enlist and do everything to the best and top of your ability."

"Thank you, Wallace."

"Did you decide not to enlist?" asked Johnny.

"I decided it was best I remained where I knew best. What better to protect than the place you grew up?"

The Corporal chimed in.

"Just stay out of our way and I won't have to question you anymore!"

"Corporal!" Wallace gave the Corporal a stern look.

The two ceased in their talking.

"Am I free to go?" asked Johnny.

"Yes, sir. You may carry on your way," said Wallace.

Johnny gave the five men a nod and headed away from them, toward Billy.

Typical P.A.W. members giving me trouble. Just because they see us as a threat due to our being more experienced in fighting than them? Not our fault my family is gifted when it comes to hand-to-hand combat.

Johnny continued in the opposite direction of the P.A.W. members. The P.A.W., or the Police Alliance of Wakesfield, the protection force for the city. Many men and women were stationed all over the city and ensured its protection.

Maybe if it weren't for that door getting stuck, they wouldn't have thought anything of it.

Johnny kept walking back toward Billy.

They take the city's protection very seriously and are seldom in the forgiving mood. There is a sense of corruption through their power, as many of the citizens do not possess any such means of power for which to stand up to them. I remember reading about them on one of the pieces of parchment in dad's room. There was lot about the history of Direfell, too.

The P.A.W. was established to keep order in the city of Wakesfield, because in the time of old, many waves ago, there was a battle, a battle so bad it became a war. The second war, also known as The Battle of the Old, was named such due to the factions fighting in it. There were many different families, such as the Hundersons, who fought amongst the enemy forces. This war took place twenty waves after the arc of peace.

If it weren't for these wars, I wonder if Wakesfield would be as protected as it is. According to some of my father's entries, from what I could read anyway, there was a beautiful time of rebuilding cities, shops, basically everything, after the first war.

Johnny continued pondering on the state of things here in Wakesfield.

If things are this bad here, then I do wonder about the state of the rest of Direfell. I know there were two wars so far . . . Declaration, the first war, and the Battle of the Old, the second war. What else could possibly be happening out there?

The Battle of the Old was sparked when a member of the Hundersons was killed. There was a pillaging of cities across Direfell and in an effort, Dumont Hunderson, someone who had enlisted in the A.C.P.F. went on a mission to stop this. He was successful at first, but the pillages kept occurring and city after city kept falling to ruin. Dumont eventually met his death, and thus, the Battle of the Old had begun.

The second war would have undoubtedly happened, regardless of whether Dumont Hunderson died. There was speculation that the pillages would have stopped had he been successful in stopping them all, thus not dying, thus no more pillaging which meant no war. On the other hand, Dumont couldn't stop all the pillaging, and this was happening in far off other lands, too, meaning that more members would have had to join forces, eventually leading to a second war.

Luckily for Johnny Hunderson, he lived in a time of relative calm—there was no war about which to worry in his homeland. If you can call being without one's family luck, then so be it. The war, however, stretched far out to the West End of Direfell, and was slowly making its way to the East End. This was why the A.C.P.F. did everything they could to stop the war from spreading anymore.

"Johnny!"

Johnny stopped his walking and turns around to see Wallace.

"Yes, Wallace?"

"Listen, one of my men just told me about your situation. I'm sorry to hear about Uncle John that way, but look, there is someone out there who knew your father."

"And you're telling me this because you think this is the man who killed him?"

"I can't say if it is or not, but he's been on our radar; back when I was first becoming a member of the P.A.W., I had heard stories about a man who would pillage lands and nearby cities," Wallace paused for a moment, "He even wound up in Wakesfield once or twice."

"Okay, Wallace, but I don't want to go after just anyone, I need to find my father's killer!"

"Johnny, this man . . . Ask around the Bulwark Bazaar about him, just . . . don't do anything stupid when you do."

Johnny gave Wallace a look.

"Listen, Johnny, all I have to give you is a nickname—he's called—"

A carrier pigeon flew aggressively in Wallace's direction. The carrier pigeon released a piece of parchment into Wallace's hand. Wallace opened up the piece of parchment and his face grew pale as he read it.

"Wallace? Wallace wait! What's his nickname?"

Wallace, who ran to respond to the urgency of the letter, shouted back to Johnny.

"Demon of the —"

Johnny could not make out the rest of what Wallace had said due to the busyness and chatter of the crowded streets.

Demon of the what? And why did Wallace run off so quickly? Has the ongoing war finally reached the doorstep of Wakesfield? As strong as I am, I don't know if I'm strong enough to fight a war should it come knocking on my doorstep. That's not a concern of mine for the time being. I do know I will be strong enough to face my father's killer, that is no question. Demon or not. As for Billy, it will be a difficult conversation when the time comes. I need to get back to him now.

Being the strong-minded person and a strong person in general, he was able to handle himself should the war really come knocking on the Stone City's doorstep. Unbeknownst to Johnny as he wasn't able to make out the legibility of these passages, his father, uncle, and his father's friends were all in the war. John Hunderson Sr. and his friends were a local platoon deployed to different regions of Direfell, such as the Fire Region or Ice Region, to rid the region of whatever troubles might be in there.

They were so good at their assignments and were famously known by many around the land. They were known as the Hunderson Gang. The group suffered their first loss when Dumont Hunderson died, which caused the Battle of the Old to happen. Twelve waves later, the Hunderson Gang suffered their second death, John Hunderson Sr. After that death, the Hunderson Gang had a falling out about who should take over, and this falling out led them to all go their separate ways.

As for his friends, they have long since ceased their fighting. They were still somewhere out there, lurking around and protecting it should things truly get out of hand. They've gone underground and shall rise again if the world truly needs them.

Johnny continued back down toward the lake, just as the sun was about to set once more. He arrived back at the lake and when he did, he headed over to Billy. At fifteen waves, Billy was already well on his way to obtaining the same achievement in his particular style of martial arts, which was the way of the Lion—there are many styles of fighting in which one can study—Billy chose this. It is a defensive style of fighting where one had a keen ability to dodge and evade attacks. This style isn't favored by many as it's seen as "weaker" as there is no true balance to it due to the lack of fighting.

Johnny assessed Billy's features, with his buzz-cut brown hair that allowed him the freedom of not having to sweep it out of his brown eyes, thereby giving him an upper hand. Billy, like all Hundersons, had the tattoo of a Black Dragon's foot on his upper right chest. Or at least he would tonight once Johnny completed the ceremony.

I hope I'm doing the right thing here. He is at the right level at his training, but it almost seems a disservice to give this to him. It really should be dad . . . My hope is that if I do it, Billy will understand that when we do find this demon, I will not be requiring his assistance. I don't want someone as weak as him to get hurt.

Billy rose to his feet and looked at Johnny.

"About time you got back. Thanks for the note. This isn't the first time you've left me alone, is it?"

Johnny continued to stare past Billy.

Billy has committed just as many waves as I have to the study of martial arts and all he got out of it was the pathetic nickname "Hunderdodge." It's a disgrace to our name.

He had a tendency to dodge attacks rather than oppose the enemy. Johnny viewed it as a sign of weakness, of cowardice. He shook his head at the idea of his younger brother wasting his time. There was no question that Johnny was better than Billy. They both knew it, but Johnny didn't lord it over Billy.

"Sorry, Billy," Johnny said with a faint smile.

"Oh, that's all right. Everything okay?"

"Yes, now come here," Johnny said calmly.

Billy moved toward Johnny. Johnny put his arm around Billy and walked him down toward the lake.

"Take your shirt off, Billy and tell me what you see."

Billy complied and took off his shirt.

"I see me, my body."

"And what don't you see? asked Johnny.

"I, uh, I don't understand. What do you mean?"

Johnny took off his shirt and stood next to Billy.

"Look in the water. My reflection. What do you see on me that is not on you?"

Billy's eyes lit up in bewilderment.

"The Black Dragon's foot tattoo! Am I getting mine tonight?!"

"You're about to find out. Now close your eyes."

Billy, who had full confidence in his brother's ability to perform the ritual correctly, closed his eyes.

Here we go, dad, this one is for you. I hope I do it justice when giving Billy this mark of our family.

Johnny placed his palm on the top right of Billy's chest and pressed, hard. He held his hand there for a moment and when he released his hand, there was now the tattoo of the Black Dragon's foot.

I did it!

"Go ahead, Billy. Open your eyes."

Billy opened his eyes and looked at his reflection in the lake.

"Now, that you have your tattoo, that doesn't mean your training ends. You must keep at it and become a master of it. You must never lose focus, otherwise . . ."

Johnny shoved Billy into the lake.

"You'll get knocked off your feet every time. Now come out of there and dry off, then get some rest."

"Are we not going to head back home, Johnny?"

"Not tonight. It's late. Get some rest."

"You're right, this was an adventure!"

Johnny smiled as Billy lays down to sleep for the night. As he does, Johnny stared at Billy, watching him as he sleeps. He continued to stare until he is sure Billy is in a deep slumber which is only a matter of moments. He then shifted his attention to the lake. Despite the gentle noises of nature making its sounds, there was a hollowness below it, like the world was below all that noise.

It's all but quiet for me; striving to find my father's killer, somewhere out there in the world. I like to think that no one was closer to him than I. He's why I am who I am. And now, at least I have more concrete information to go on, thanks to Wallace.

Johnny sat down by the lake and pulled out the pieces of parchment from his bag, and scoured them for information about anything having to do with a demon.

Demon. Demon. What's this here? The Forest Region . . . the biggest region of them all? I wonder, in a place as big as this, could this demon be stirring here? Wallace did say the demon used to come to Wakesfield, and this is the closest region to here.

Johnny put the map down for a moment, looked back at Billy, then picked back up the map again.

This really will be an adventure . . . This trip is no light feat. Just getting out of Wakesfield will prove difficult. I don't know what these three markings here, but there are names written. Waning. Watchful. Wander. If it has to do with the P.A.W. then that's even more trouble.

Hours passed as Johnny sat and stared glancing over these maps and pieces of information gathered from the parchment. He once more looked back at Billy who was in a deep slumber due to his almost lifeless body.

This is it; we can take this route here to get out of the city. All the avenues and roads on this map of Wakesfield all lead back to these three 'w's. This must be the only way to leave.

Johnny looked back out at the lake, reminiscing about when he was last seeking information and why no one told him about this demon. A scowl took over his blank face. He shook it off, turned around and looked at Billy once more. He approached him and woke him up.

"Billy."

Billy slowly stirred in his sleep.

"Billy, wake up!"

Tired and confused, Billy slowly opened his eyes. He realized it is Johnny who spoke to him. He sat up and faced Johnny.

"What is it, Johnny? I'm trying to sleep."

"Today is the day we go on our big adventure."

Billy rubbed his eyes.

"What do you mean?"

"The letter I received. Remember the letter?"

Billy sat completely still as he became mesmerized by Johnny's words.

"For the past few hours I've been sitting here looking through these maps from Dad's room—"

"You went into dad's room?"

"Yes, Billy, I'll explain everything, just listen."

"I got these maps from dad's room and they have a lot of information on them," Johnny said pausing with a confused look appearing on his face, "Most of which is hard to make out, but that's not the point."

"I would hope not," said Billy with a touch of sarcasm.

"Look. Here. There's a region out here called the Forest Region and I believe this might be home to the demon Wallace was telling me about."

"Slow down, Johnny, you saw Wallace and he's a demon? "

"No. Just, no more questions. Let me explain, please."

Billy nodded in agreement.

"Wallace told me about how he just heard about our father's death, and he had a piece of information to pass along to me. A name. Before he could get the full name out, he was summoned to handle a matter. Regardless, the name I got is a nickname, the 'Demon of the' and that's all I have. I also ran into Thomas when I had left you here the other day and he was mentioning the Bulwark Bazaar and I think we need to go there! A lot of people roaming Direfell pass through there and it should be a great place to get more information."

Billy stared at Johnny, too timid for once to have said anything.

"I'm finished, Billy."

"Okay, so, we need to get to the Bulwark Bazaar?"

"Yes."

"Okay, then let's get going!"

"Listen, Billy, I want you to go home and wait there where it's safe."

"What? No way! I'm coming with you and there's nothing you can do to stop me."

"There's a lot I can do to stop you, actually, but that's beside the point. I don't want you to get in my way."

"I won't. I promise. You promised me an adventure."

"That I did," said Johnny pausing for a moment. "I just wanted to make sure you were up for it."

He really is relentless. If I do find this demon, how am I going to convince Billy to stay behind?

"You said it yourself. I have the Black Dragon's foot tattoo now," said Billy, "I'm not going to lose my focus. Let's go!"

A smile appeared across Johnny's face as the two of them gathered and packed up their gear and headed back toward Coheod Market and exited out of the unkept orchard area. As they did the sun had shown itself once more.

"I can't believe we're leaving Wakesfield," said Billy.

"We need information on that first. This is why we're heading back to the market, but we'll have to make it quick. The P.A.W. is onto my heckling merchants for information."

As both Johnny and Billy arrived to the Coheod Market, the sun was now in the center of the sky, and it shone bright.

"I can never seem to get over how long that walk takes," said Billy.

"Been doing it since we were kids."

"I know, but still."

"Don't complain about walking when we're going to be walking through the rest of the city and for the rest of this adventure," replied Johnny.

The two of them continued their approach to Coheod Market.

"What are we going to do, Johnny?" asked Billy.

"We're going to the Forest Region, Billy. We're going to track down our father's killer and—"

"And what?" asked Billy.

"And bring him to justice," said Johnny, adjusting his gear, "Now let's get a move on."

"What about supplies? We have to return home first to pack."

"I've already done that, Billy."

"You did what? When did you leave?"

"When you were sleeping."

Billy gave Johnny a look of disdain.

"This isn't the first time you've roamed off, is it?" asked Billy. "I asked you this earlier and you didn't answer."

"I'm afraid not. However, I needed answers and I did not wish to inconvenience you."

"Inconvenience me? The only inconvenience was your note. Who leaves a note saying 'be back soon'?"

"I mean it's true. I came back soon."

The two of them shared a small chuckle. They arrived at Coheod Market; it was late afternoon. Johnny approached one of the vendors.

"Hey there, how goes it."

"Good afternoon, sir, what will it be?"

"Just a piece of information. If I'm to make leave from this city and head to the Forest Region, which way should I go?"

"D—did you say the Forest Region?"

"Yes."

The merchant's face went cold as his eyes widened with panic and fear.

"Is there a problem, merchant?"

"There's a reason I took my business elsewhere. I don't even want to think about that region . . ."

"What's so bad about it?" asked Johnny.

"Leave my stand! I do not wish to talk about this. Or am I going to have to notify the police?"

Johnny looked over his shoulder and saw the P.A.W. members who patrolled this area.

"That won't be necessary, I'll just take my business elsewhere."

Johnny grabbed Billy by the arm and the two of them quickly moved up the street to a different merchant.

"Hey there, I'll make this quick. What can you tell me about the Forest Region?"

"Help, please help! I'm being robbed!" shouted the merchant.

"You there. Halt!" shouted a member of the P.A.W.

Johnny looked at Billy.

"Run!"

Both Johnny and Billy ran as fast as they can, and headed even farther down the street, with the members of the P.A.W. in pursuit.

"Here!"

Johnny shoved Billy into the crowd on the left side of the street while Johnny blended in on the right. Members of the P.A.W. arrived moments later and came to a halt. One stepped forward and let out a commanding voice.

"Citizens of Wakesfield! We are seeking two men travelling together, harassing merchants and trying to rob them. If you are to see them, please notify a member of P.A.W. That is all. Return to your lives, citizens."

Johnny continued slinking through the crowds of people, weaving in and out. He approached a cross section in the road and locked eyes with Billy, then shook his head. The two of them continued moving down Coheod Market.

"Excuse me, sir?" said a man to Johnny, placing his hand on his shoulder.

Johnny turned around, worried to whom he'd see when he did.

"Yes?" asked Johnny.

"So sorry, sir, I was wondering if you had the time?"

Johnny's face went blank before he rolled his eyes then pointed upward to the giant clock tower, with its blaring ticking noise, which permeated the whole city.

"Ah, yes, so sorry! Have a good day."

"You as well," said Johnny, cautiously.

"Oh, and by the way . . . anyone who enters the Forest Region has never come back out."

"Wait, what? Come back!" shouted Johnny, as the man disappears into the crowd.

And just who was that? Obviously someone was watching me. He knows I can't chase him down or shout too loudly without alerting the P.A.W. I need to catch back up with Billy.

Johnny turned the corner and bumped into Billy.

"Watch where you're—oh, it's you."

"Yeah, sorry, I was distracted, Billy."

"Seeing as we're under pursuit by the P.A.W., I can see why."

"We need to get out of here, still. Far out of here."

"Johnny, you aren't the least bit concerned that people are afraid to talk about the Forest Region?" asked Billy.

"Why would I be?" asked Johnny, before he continued speaking, "Well, someone did just say something to me . . ."

"What? What is it that they said?" asked Billy, raising an eyebrow.

"Anyone who entered the Forest Region has never come back out."

Billy gave Johnny a blank stare at first, then his eyes widened with fear.

"Johnny, you can't be serious about going in there then can you?"

"I must. I have no choice!"

"Yes you do! Why don't we recruit some people to help us?"

"Where?"

"Like the bazaar! There must be people there," said Billy.

"No. This is something to do alone."

"Can we at least look?"

"Look where?" asked Johnny.

"I don't know, here in Wakesfield?"

"I'm not spending any more time here than we have to. If the

P.A.W. catches up with us, we're done for. They're going to detain us for questioning and that's time we don't have."

"Okay, what about the other regions? You mentioned the Forest Region so there must be other regions out there, right?" asked Billy.

"Yes, and if the need so arises, I will assemble a group of people I can trust. However, I don't see that happening . . . it's just one person out there who I'm after." said Johnny, firmly.

"What if there are other evils in the world like there are regions? There are other regions, correct?"

"Yes, you're correct. So the map said." Johnny replied, ignoring Billy's first question.

"Then why not look in the other regions before going to the Forest Region if it's so dangerous?" asked Billy.

"The other regions? The only way to get to those other regions is by going *through* the Forest Region."

"We could always go around it."

"You have no concept of how big the Forest Region is, do you, Billy?"

"Do you?!" Billy shouted.

"Billy, relax."

"Johnny, you're going to drive me insane! You want to go find answers and I do, too, but I can't believe the lack of planning."

"Lack of planning?" asked Johnny.

"I just feel you're not thinking clearly."

"Billy, for the first time I am thinking clearly—I've never thought about something more than I have thought about this adventure."

"Adventure? Adventures are meant to be fun, Johnny. This sounds like a suicide mission."

Billy stared at Johnny with great concern.

"Nevertheless, I want to go with you. You're all I have left right now since our brothers are in the war."

Billy let out a big sigh, then looked at Johnny.

"Let me know when this adventure is beginning, at least."

"Now."

"Now, what?" asked Billy.

"The adventure begins."

"When you promised me an adventure, I didn't think this was going to be it."

Chapter 5

"Wasn't it just late afternoon a moment ago?" asked Billy. Johnny looked around and realized this is the shadowy street which he saw earlier.

"This is it."

Johnny moved farther down the street as the world's sound around him became distant and faint. It wasn't until Billy walked up to Johnny and put his hand on his shoulder that Johnny stopped inching forward, moving downward toward the street's middle.

"Johnny, what are you doing? You're getting lost in this trance . . . Knock it off."

"Don't you hear it, Billy?"

"I'm gonna ask 'hear what?' which would indicate my obvious response that I do in fact hear nothing. Absolutely nothing."

"Exactly! I hear nothing, too! The world around me seems to have stopped and my heart has begun beating faster—I was beginning to sweat and get flushed."

Billy smirked and, with his hand still on Johnny's shoulder, turned him around and looked at him chuckling.

"Sounds like you're in love. Did you see a pretty lady down that street?"

"No, I—I don't know what I saw. I—It was just darkness . . . Emptiness . . . Nothingness . . . Loneliness . . ."

"Distractedness," commented Billy jokingly, "Now let's go."

"Right. Go. Yeah, we're off to the Bulwark Bazaar."

"Johnny, this is exactly what I mean, you're so distracted and I just feel—"

"Well, I'm happy that you feel, but your feelings aren't going to change my mind."

Billy just looked at Johnny. He adjusted his straps on his bag and began walking away from Johnny.

"Well, come on then. Let's go!" said Billy.

"On the map it was just a thick black line. This must correlate to this street."

Johnny glanced once more down the street.

"I suppose we can always revisit this place later," said Johnny, faintly.

Both Johnny and Billy walked away from the shadowy street with its terminable end—which resided simply a few yards down. There was a giant dumpster on the left wall, which rose high into the sky, and then on the right wall there was nothing that Johnny could see. This street was simply covered in shadow and darkness and its end was visibly seen—it's just like being underneath two large trees in the afternoon when the sun was high up and shining bright, there was no light underneath the two trees. Just a large, covered area of shadow and shade.

There must be something more to this street, there just has to be.

As Johnny and Billy made their way out of the shadowy street, a man passed both of them and bumped into Johnny.

"Excuse me, sir."

"Excuse me—wait a minute! Billy, that's the guy who told me about the Forest Region!"

The man who bumped into the brothers began to run down the street and Johnny took off after him.

"Johnny, wait!"

Billy began to chase after Johnny.

"Come back here, you!" Johnny shouted, chasing the man.

Johnny reached the end of the shadowy street where the dumpster was. He looked all over, high and low, and saw no trace of the man.

It's as if he just disappeared into thin air.

"Johnny, you okay?" asked Billy.

"Yes, sorry about that. Usually I don't go causing a scene like that chasing off after someone, but no one would be able to hear us anyway. I have a feeling there's a lot more to this street than we're seeing."

"What do you mean?"

"I haven't seen this street marked anywhere on the map of Wakesfield. It has to be that thick black line."

"Maybe dad never came to this street," said Billy.

"Oh come on, he travels around all of Direfell, in and out of Wakesfield and he doesn't mark this one street? No, there's something different going on here."

Johnny knelt on one knee and felt the ground with his fingers, he ran them across the cobblestone street.

It's just like any other street, except it doesn't seem to be any normal street.

Johnny, with a confused face, looked quietly back at Billy.

"What is it, Johnny?"

"Feel the stone."

Billy knelt on one knee and he, too, felt the ground with his fingers, and ran them across the cobblestone street.

55

"What do you feel?" asked Johnny.

"It feels like any other normal street, but it . . . doesn't."

Johnny looked at Billy who paused for a moment in his speech.

"Does that make sense, Johnny?"

"I thought the same thing. The stone almost feels . . . wet, like there's this movement to it."

As they both rose back to their feet, they started walking back toward the main drag of Wakesfield. As they did, they heard voices coming from a distance.

"Citizens of Wakesfield! We are seeking two men travelling together, harassing merchants and trying to rob them. If you are to see them, please notify a member of P.A.W. That is all. Return to your lives, citizens."

"Geez, the P.A.W. doesn't give up, do they?" questions Billy.

"All the more reason for us to get out of the city, now," replied Johnny.

"We have to be careful!"

"We do. We also have to come back to this street sometime in the future. There's got to be more to it, I just know it!"

As they edged closer back to the main drag of Wakesfield, they saw a female member of the P.A.W. who questioned a merchant.

"You mean to tell me you've been here *all day*, merchant, but haven't sold anything?"

"T—that's correct. It's a very busy market," said the merchant, nervously.

The female member of the P.A.W. grabbed the merchant and pinned him down against his cart. She pulled out her locking cuffs and linked the merchant's hands together.

"It's not me, I swear! I would never harass my fellow merchants."

"You're coming with us for questioning. What better place to hide than in plain view?"

As the merchant was dragged away, he spotted both Johnny and Billy.

"There they are! See, I told you I'm not one of them!"

More members of the P.A.W. arrived to investigate, but as they did, Johnny and Billy made a mad dash to get away.

"Johnny!"

"Yes, Billy, just keep moving."

"Which way!?"

"Just follow me!"

The two of them ran in the opposite direction of the P.A.W.

"Doesn't that map have a secret passage we can take or something?" asked Billy.

As Johnny and Billy kept running, they passed by people and various merchants and streets, Johnny saw something that caught his eye.

"There! This is the street we need to go down. Move!"

Both Johnny and Billy made their way quickly down the street and took cover behind the numerous dumpsters. Johnny took out the map of Wakesfield and examined it.

"We're very close, Billy."

"Close to what?"

"The map shows here another part of Wakesfield called Britlas Row. It's just past this warning line here on the map."

"Warning line?" asked Billy.

"Yeah, it's just a long line through the map and it said warning."

"Warning usually implies something dangerous, Johnny."

"It just probably means to warn us that we're leaving one part of Wakesfield and headed for another. Maybe these lines represent jurisdiction for different rankings of the P.A.W."

"Here's hoping."

Johnny put the map back into his bag and slung the bag over his shoulder. The two of them peeked out from behind the dumpster, then continued down the street.

"Drink some water, Billy. We've done a lot of running and we need to make sure if the need to run rises again, we'll be well replenished. Grab a bite to eat, too."

"Won't you be doing the same, Johnny?"

"Don't worry about me, Billy, I'll be fine."

"But I do worry about you," said Billy, softly and under his breath, inaudible to Johnny.

The two of them continued making their way toward Britlas Row, leaving Coheod Market far behind in the distance. As they kept making way, the sun began to set once more. Johnny wiped the sweat from his forehead, but that sweat does not compare to the cold sweat he just felt as the first lamppost that lit and illuminated the brothers.

"Billy, we need to move. Quickly."

Johnny and Billy continued walking faster, instead of jogging or running, as to not arouse any suspicion.

"It's darker."

"Yes, Johnny, the lampposts."

"No, I mean, up ahead . . . it's much . . . darker. There are no more lampposts this way. We must be getting close!"

Johnny and Billy trekked forward on their adventure.

"What else did you see in dad's journal?" asked Billy.

"Oh, uh, well most of it was illegible, but there were many interesting things in it."

"Like what?"

"Okay, here's one, it almost reads like some legend. I couldn't make all of it out, but the passage was titled the 'Enchanted Eye Entities.'"

"That sounds interesting!" exclaimed Billy.

"Surely does, even more so were the pages that followed."

"Okay, so what are the Enchanted Eye Entities?" asked Billy.

"Well, as far as I can tell, they're some mythical, magical beings who roam Direfell somewhere with special powers, I'm not so sure. Like I said, it reads more like a legend than it does anything real."

"Do you think there are magical things out there in Direfell?"

"I hadn't given it much thought, Billy, but after seeing that shadowy street, I'm open to believing a lot of things. It's just like Wallace was telling me about the demon and how it used to pillage the nearby cities and villages."

"I didn't even know there *were* any other cities or villages outside of Wakesfield," commented Billy.

"Nor did I, not until I saw this map that is. And even so . . . I still don't see much of anything in terms of villages, let alone cities."

"They must be tiny then."

"Any city compared to Wakesfield is going to be tiny. I can't possibly imagine a bigger city, I mean it takes us a full day just to get through Coheod Market and then some. Speaking of which, we need to find a good, dark area to make rest for the night. Whatever this Britlas Row is, I want to be ready."

"Agreed."

Johnny and Billy continued walking hurriedly down the increasingly dimming part of Wakesfield and looked for an enclosed area where they can rest. They both laid down and closed their eyes and allowed their heartbeats to return to a normal beating pattern and for the adrenaline to have worn off. The moon rose into the sky as the sun finally set. The moon's glow beamed off a mass amount of light, but Johnny and Billy made sure they picked an area where the moon's glow wouldn't shed any light on them, or at least not much.

As the two brothers were deep into their sleep, there was a loud, rumbling sound, followed by a bright light that permeated the nearby streets, close to the brothers. Soon to follow, there was another rumbling sound, this one more akin to a hissing noise.

Johnny stirred and heard this noise, thinking it is part of some lucid dream, before realizing the sound was getting closer. His eyes shot open as he took in his surroundings.

What is that sound?

Johnny slowly rose to a crouched position and peered out from behind the dumpster and looked around the corner.

Oh no . . .

What Johnny just saw was an entire platoon of members of the P.A.W. testing their new devices. In the world of Direfell, things moved rather quickly, and new inventions were constantly being created. This particular invention was a flare. It was loud in its rumbling and as scintillating as the sun at high noon.

"Light these streets up! We need to find our quarry. We mustn't let them get out of this city," commanded a member of the P.A.W.

Johnny slowly made his way back to Billy and shook him lightly, but continuously, until he woke up.

"Billy, we need to move. Now."

Billy, still sleepy, slowly got up, until he heard a sound of another flare being struck and cast to the ground which lit up the street.

"What was that noise, Johnny?"

Before Johnny had a chance to answer, a flare was thrown by a member of the P.A.W. and landed at the edge of the street the brothers were in. Billy and Johnny quickly covered their eyes due to the flare's blinding glow.

"I don't know, but we need to go!"

Both blindly grabbed their gear by way of touch and opened their eyes to a squinted view and made their way down the street, into the cover of darkness.

"Are we close, Johnny? Because you keep saying we're close to Britlas Row and I haven't seen any signs indicating we're there."

Johnny stopped dead in his tracks, with Billy almost bumping into Johnny as he did.

"Why'd you stop so suddenly?"

"That . . ."

Johnny and Billy stared in bewilderment.

"You were wondering why you didn't see any signs, that's why. This isn't a line at all," said Johnny.

Before both Johnny and Billy stood a wall of insurmountable height. The wall's length stretched on as far down as the brothers could see. Johnny glanced down at the map.

"This line extends the entirety of the city, from left to right."

"How are we going to get over it?" asked Billy.

"I don't know, but I do know our grappling hooks aren't long enough to scale that. Even if we used the ropes from both grappling hooks to extend it into one long grappling hook."

"What do we do?" asked Billy.

"There must be a way through. How else would anyone ever get in or out of this city?"

"Maybe that's exactly why this wall is here, Johnny, so no one can get out."

Johnny looked at Billy with a look one would give if they found out they failed a test.

"*Walls.*"

"Excuse me?" asked Billy.

"That's what the lines on this map represent. Walls. Three of them."

Chapter 6

"Three walls?" asked Billy.

"Yes, Billy. Three walls. Three walls stand before us and our exit from this city, from the answers we so desperately crave to find our father's killer."

"Not just three walls, Johnny, look!"

Johnny looked over to where Billy had just motioned.

"Members of the P.A.W. patrol these walls. Of course."

The walls placed in Wakesfield were barriers to keep people in and people out—not to segregate in any way, just as added security. Each wall was guarded heavily by members of the P.A.W. Easily distinguished by their uniforms—a dark blue tunic fitted with pauldrons to cover and protect the shoulders, vambraces down the forearms, and greaves covering the legs. Tied around the waist of the tunic was a black belt with a few pouches in the back, with a special pouch created for holding the locking cuffs.

On the one side of the belt was a holder for a baton, and in it rested the baton. This weapon would easily maim an attacker if enough force was applied. It would even knock someone out flat, or worse, kill them if hit in the head near the temple. On the right was a holder for a blade, and in it rested the blade. The blade would be used in the most serious of matters where the baton could not do justice to stop an attacker. Of course, while simply knocking one out with the baton would put a stop to the attacker, they couldn't be questioned until they'd come to.

I can't believe we have to not only get past a wall, but past an unknown number of the P.A.W.

"Let's go, Billy. We just need to follow along this wall until we find some sort of door or something."

The two of them made their move and got closer to the wall, only this time, they walked in the opposite direction the P.A.W. walked.

Maybe we can get some sort of key from one of them if we can spot one with a key.

"What's the plan, Johnny?"

"Just keep moving, keep cool, and keep your head down."

"And keep my focus," said Billy with a light heart.

"Yes, Billy. Always keep your focus."

Johnny and Billy walked down along the wall, hoping to find some sort of door or ladder to allow them access to the other side.

These walls were large in height, width, and made entirely of stone. This was a special kind of stone that was impervious to all sorts of drilling, meddling, and other schemes. This was due to a special kind of stone invented to be able to withstand certain attacks like fire or earthquakes. In case another war was to reach Wakesfield, the P.A.W. wanted to be ready, so they studied the different tactics and had these walls constructed. The only way to get past these walls was to get past the P.A.W. Doing this was not an easy feat, but there were always ways around if one knew their way around.

"Johnny, how are we even supposed to get past this wall? Not to even mention the other walls."

Clarity hit Johnny as he replied, "Family, Billy. Family is all that matters, and it's all that ever will."

As Johnny and Billy kept walking, they saw a platoon of P.A.W. members standing around, keeping guard. Both Johnny and Billy moved closer toward the platoon, who seemingly guarded nothing. Next to the platoon, they saw a stand where there were a multitude of pigeons, sitting around.

"Carrier pigeons. This must be it."

"Johnny, what do we do?"

"Just relax."

"But what if they recognize us from that merchant earlier?"

"Billy, you're losing your focus. Remember what happens next if you lose your focus."

Billy nodded and the two of them inch closer toward the door.

"The best thing to do, as you know, is to hide in plain sight. Let them see us," said Johnny.

"Let them see us? Are you crazy?" asked Billy.

Johnny approached the door, and he was instantly stopped by a P.A.W. member.

"This is Wall One. What business do you have trying to leave through this door, young man?" asked a member of P.A.W.

"Family," replied Johnny, "We're on our way to see family."

"Hmm, what is your last name, boy?"

"Hunderson."

"And this person with you?" asked Wall One.

"Hunderson as well, he's my brother," replied Johnny.

The P.A.W. member studied both Johnny and Billy.

"State your reason for departure."

"As aforementioned, sir, we're leaving to go visit family. They're on the other side of Wakesfield and we need passage through these walls."

"Their names?" asked Wall One.

"We tend to be private people," replied Johnny.

"Then no access will be granted. Step back, please."

Johnny paused for a moment before responding to the member of the P.A.W.

"We're off to see Wallace Ecallaw."

"Wallace Ecallaw. *You're* off to see Wallace?" asked Wall One.

"Yes, sir, he's our cousin," responded Johnny.

"Wallace Ecallaw, your *cousin*, is my commanding officer. I shall just dispatch a notice ahead to clarify."

Johnny looked back at Billy and smiled. The member of P.A.W. grabbed a piece of parchment and began writing down a note coded so only other members of P.A.W. could read it.

The P.A.W. member finished writing the message and called for a carrier pigeon. The pigeon flew to the man's arm and got the note attached to a little note holder on the pigeon's foot. The man then sent off the pigeon.

As the pigeon flew away up into the sky, both Johnny and Billy watched in amazement. There was a long pause between the brothers and the P.A.W. member to whom they just spoke.

"A long time for something that's a such a sure thing," said Wall One.

Just then, another member of P.A.W. walked up to Wall One and whispered something to him. Wall One's eyes widened and instantly shifted to both Johnny and Billy.

A cold sweat ran down both Johnny and Billy's necks as they stood there, wondering why they had caught the gaze of Wall One.

Another member of P.A.W. walked up to the platoon and Wall One.

"What's going on here, sergeant?"

"I have two kids here stating they wish to be granted passage through the wall to see their cousin Wallace," responded Wall One.

"Wallace? Wallace Ecallaw?"

"Yes, sir. They claim to be his cousin," stated Wall One.

"It's not a claim, sir, it is in fact the truth," interrupted Johnny.

After there was yet another long pause between all parties, a carrier pigeon flew down and landed on Wall One's extended arm. He pulled out the message from the pigeon's carrier, opened it, and read it over. He then reached to his side, where his baton was.

Both Johnny and Billy stood completely frozen and stared at Wall One. What Wall One grabbed is instead of his baton is a key—this was not just any ordinary key, though, this key was huge and was for the first wall that granted access to Britlas Row.

"Green light."

Wall One placed the key on the wall and a giant stone door formed from the wall in front of Johnny and Billy, then opened slowly.

"Gentlemen, go ahead. Access to Death Row granted."

"*Death* Row? Don't you mean *Britlas* Row?" asked Johnny, raising an eyebrow.

"There's . . . there's nothing here?" said Billy, confused.

"Why do you think we nickname this place Death Row?" said Wall One, letting out a boisterous laugh.

Both Johnny and Billy entered through the door. As quickly as they entered was as quickly as the door shut behind them and formed back into the wall.

Chapter 7

As Johnny and Billy moved a few steps forward, to their immediate right, they saw a tattered sign with the word 'Britlas' crossed out and over it written the word 'Death'.

"Death row, eh?" asked Billy, "Why do you suppose they call it that?" Billy asked sarcastically.

"Look at this place . . . there's nothing . . . there's no one here."

Johnny and Billy took a moment to look all around them and take in their surroundings.

"This place looks like it used to be full of life, but now . . . now there's this emptiness to it, just like that shadowy street back at Coheod Market."

"Yeah what was up with that street, Johnny?"

"I don't know, but this must all somehow be connected."

The brothers walked away from the first wall and left it behind in the distance.

"Everywhere I look I see tattered lampposts, broken benches, and worn-down buildings," said Johnny, "If things in Direfell are as bad as they are here in Wakesfield, then maybe there is something bigger going on out there."

"Our brothers are still off fighting in the war," said Billy

"Yes but could it have already hit Wakesfield?" asked Johnny as he separated from Billy and continued to look around.

No, this can't be the same war. This is something different; something older, but what?

"Hey, Johnny!"

Johnny turned to where Billy was standing and walked back over to him.

"Yeah what is it?"

"Well, that wasn't so bad, eh?"

"That was only wall one, Billy."

"Okay, so what?"

"So what? Just a moment ago you were so concerned about us making it through. And now that we have, you think it's easy street? Far from it, Billy."

Johnny pulled out the map of Wakesfield from his bag and examined it.

"If these lines represent walls then these scribblings next to each line must be some kind of name, but I can't make it out."

"Here, let me take a look!"

Billy examined the map closely and squinted his eyes as he tried to make out the words.

"This first one said 'Warning.'"

"Warning?" asked Johnny.

"Yes, Warning. These other ones are named Waning and Watchful."

"So, the three walls each have their own name, and each more daunting than the last," stated Johnny.

"What do you suppose those names mean, Johnny?"

"It means we have our work cut out for us. These walls aren't that easy to slip past, and while I'm glad we made it past this one, I'm not too sure of the difficulties that lay ahead."

The two of them continued walking.

"Warning Wall . . . that must mean that the wall is warning us of things to come? How the wall will lead to emptiness? But then why call the next one Waning Wall? It must be due to the nature of the wall, or its state after what happened to this place."

"You think it's falling apart?" asked Billy.

"By very definition, it would be fading away, so yes, something to that effect."

Johnny and Billy continued down the cobblestone road, while their mud-brown boots clogged underneath them and kicked up whiffs of small stones as they did. This part of Wakesfield was ghost-quiet; its inhabitants were non-existent in this part of the Stone City and had no inhabitants in waves. When the first war, Declaration, struck the land, Wakesfield was used as a stronghold and the evil forces of the world pushed back its defendants all the way to their penultimate wall. Due to this, there was destruction and the buildings have not been touched or rebuilt—this part of the land remained empty and merely as a passing point for those who wished to exit the city.

"Why did that guard say they nicknamed this place 'Death Row'? Sure, there is no one here from what we've seen, but death? Really?"

"Maybe people that make it past the first wall don't ever make it to the second," said Billy.

"Yes, and because there is no market here from the looks of it, they must die."

Johnny cross-referenced this part of Wakesfield from what he read in his father's journal.

"It didn't make sense to me before, but it does now . . . I read in dad's journal that there was a holding point somewhere in Wakesfield. This must be it!"

Britlas Row, more commonly known as Death Row, was just that. A holding point for those who made it past the first wall but could make it past the second. In Wakesfield, you're not allowed to return to the city until your stated business is complete. For example, if going on a hunting trip that was meant to last for two bits and your party returned in one, they must wait one full bit outside of the walls of Wakesfield until they're granted access again.

As Johnny and Billy continued down the stretch of road, they arrived at what appears to be some sort of town.

"This looks like the place that time forgot," said Billy

All around them were worn-down buildings, tattered merchant stands, and scraps of food scattered around the area. There were also a few people who aimlessly wandered around the area, too, that meandered and interacted with the scraps of food.

Johnny approached one of these people.

"Excuse me, miss? Can you tell me what happened here?"

The girl looked up at Johnny with a crazed look in her eyes. She then murmured something to Johnny.

"One more bit, one more bit, one more bit, yes, one more bit until I'm allowed back in to Wakesfield."

Johnny pulled out his water and offered the girl some. She gladly accepted and almost snatched the canteen from Johnny's hand that held it over her mouth. As the water escaped the canteen and entered her parched mouth, she smiled.

"Thank you, thank you, thank you, yes, one bit until I'm allowed back into Wakesfield."

Johnny stepped back from the girl, retrieved his canteen, and put it away.

"Something is seriously wrong here, Billy."

"You're telling me."

"We've gone for days without food while on those hunting trips with dad and we never succumbed to this type of delusion."

"Exactly! Sure, we were famished, but we still had our wits about us for the most part."

"I remember feeling a little groggy, albeit hungry, but not like this . . . this is something different. Someone did something to these people here."

Johnny and Billy advanced closer toward the frayed market. Johnny approached a crate and stepped on top of it.

"Citizens of Wakesfield, what happened here? Who did this to you?"

"Johnny, what are you doing?"

"I may be focused on finding dad's killer, but that doesn't mean we can turn our backs on those in need. Plus, they may have some information on the Forest Region."

"I agree wholeheartedly, Johnny, but these people are lost. Crazed! They need food. They need help! If we can make it the next wall, we can ask the P.A.W. for help."

Johnny looked back at Billy.

"I think it's the P.A.W. who did this, Billy."

A man approached Johnny and took a swipe at him. Johnny was quick to react and jumped back off the crate.

"You're one of them, aren't you? You're a member of the P.A.W.!"

"No, I assure you, I'm not," responded Johnny to the man.

"Two days! TWO DAYS!" said the man, now screaming at Johnny.

"Maybe you're right, Billy. Let's go get them help."

"You're not going anywhere!" said the man who previously swiped at Johnny.

The man took another swipe at Johnny, this time he stepped forward as he did. Johnny, once again was quick to react and swatted down the man's hand.

"I don't want to fight any of you, please. Allow us safe passage through here and we shall do what we can do help!" exclaimed Johnny.

"Give us all of your food and you can go through," said one man to Johnny.

"We need this food as we continue our trek to reach the Waning Wall," responded Johnny.

"Too bad! Looks like you're going to have to fight us after all."

Two men charged at Johnny, their hands clenched into fists aimed for his face. Johnny raised both of his forearms and blocked the incoming punches. He was then quick to grab both men by their respective arms and he swung them into one another, then shoved them back.

"I don't have time for this! I do not wish to fight anyone but the person who killed my father. Now please, all of you, back off!" shouted Johnny, sternly.

The two men who attacked Johnny cowered in fear, as the other men and woman there went back and scrounged through the scraps.

"Thank you," said Johnny, as he grabbed Billy by the arm and quickly left.

"What was that, Johnny?"

"What was what, Billy?"

"One minute you're saying you shouldn't turn your back on those people and the next minute we're leaving."

Johnny stopped dead in his tracks and turned to face Billy.

"Don't ever question my morals again. Got that?"

Billy's eyes widened with fear.

"I just meant . . . this mission is going to consume you, Johnny. I fear it already has."

"Look, Billy, I want nothing more than to find our father's killer, and I don't want anything or anyone standing in our way."

"Even an unsurmountable obstacle?" asked Billy.

"An obstacle only remains an obstacle until you push it out of the way," replied Johnny, as he turned away from Billy and continued walking.

"Come on, we'll walk for just a moment longer to get away from everyone back there, then we'll set up and sleep for the night."

"All right, Johnny."

Johnny and Billy strolled for about another two hours and made sure to give enough space between them and the people back in the torn market, before they set up camp for the night.

When morning arrived, the brothers were quick to pack up their belongings and continued their travels. As they did, they saw a man talking to a wall and another man seated across from him. He hugged his knees and rocked back and forth, while he murmured something.

"What do you suppose he's saying?" asked Billy.

"Only one way to find out . . ."

"Johnny, wait!"

Johnny approached the man cradling his knees and knelt down next to him.

"What's that you're saying?"

The man slowly raised his head. His eyes were partly open, and he had bags underneath his eyes of a plum purple color. His beard was sandy brown and smelled of bit-old trash. He struggled to open his mouth as his lips were as dry as the desert from which he came. Johnny pulled out his water and handed him some.

"Th-thank you, sir," said the man.

"You're welcome. Now, would you mind telling me why you were looking at my brother and me?"

"You mean . . . you don't . . ."

"Don't what?" asked Johnny.

Johnny looked down at this man's clothing. He was in a uniform.

"Who are you?" asked Johnny.

"The darkness is coming. Sand Region. The world is getting darker . . . there is an approaching shadow and there is nothing we can do to stop it. They're too strong. They are very skilled."

"Who? Who are *they?*"

"They're coming. We can't stop them . . ."

The man's eyes closed shut and he fell slowly over. Johnny stood up and took a few steps back. He lowered his head as a sign of respect for this man who passed, then made his way back over to Billy.

"What happened?"

"He's dead, Billy."

"What? What was he saying?"

"He kept saying that darkness is coming. I don't know."

"Johnny, you're the last person to miss a word someone said; you're always paying attention, thinking multiple steps ahead of everyone else. Now, what did he say?"

"That there is an approaching shadow."

Johnny paused and looked at Billy, then looked back at the man.

I wonder if he is talking about the street I passed by earlier. That shadowy street: if he is, then maybe it's best both Billy and I exit Wakesfield. Not just for our adventure, but for our safety as well. If something or someone is coming, Billy and I aren't strong enough to face it. We really will need help . . . That man was a member of the A.C.P.F., and if he was worried, then maybe we should be, too.

Johnny stood incredibly still.

I must first take down my father's killer. Doing such will make me stronger and ready. I am ready.

"Billy, we're moving on. Let's go."

Billy looked at Johnny with an inquisitive look on his face. Billy knew Johnny was just deep in thought as he had that look on his face . . . that look that one gives when asked when they're going to stop wetting the bed, or if a tree falls in the middle of the forest, does it make a sound.

"What is it, Johnny?"

"I can't shake what that man said. It almost felt like this matter was happening today."

"Is it?"

"I can't be too sure. I just have this odd feeling like I knew him somehow . . . I just . . ."

The Sand Region . . . where is this?

Johnny pulled out the map detailing Direfell and searched it for the Sand Region.

"Here it is, Billy. The Sand Region. This is what this man was saying."

"What about the Sand Region?"

"He was saying how there's darkness there and how it's making its way to the rest of Direfell," said Johnny.

"Where *is* the Sand Region?"

Johnny pointed to it on the map and showed Billy.

"It looks like it's way out East . . . well beyond Wakesfield."

"Beyond Wakesfield?" asked Billy.

"Yes."

"I didn't even think anything was out past Wakesfield on the East End of Direfell."

"It doesn't look like there is, but there's all of this sand scattered around this one area with a marking saying Sand Region. Whether or not this is the exact location or just an approximate one is beyond my knowledge."

"What good is that map being marked if we still don't know what or where something is?" asked Billy.

"Never mind that now. We're heading west toward the city limits then due south toward the Bulwark Bazaar. Unless it pertains to our father's death, I've no interest in discussing the Sand Region anymore. We need to stay focused on the task at hand. Making it past the Waning Wall."

Johnny and Billy made their way closer to the second wall. The emptiness made this trek seem interminable, like one who tried to find where one ocean ended, and another began.

After a few hours, the brothers saw a familiar setting in the distance. A platoon of P.A.W. guarded a wall. There was something eerily different about this particular platoon, though. It was not until the brothers approached too closely that they discovered just exactly what that difference is.

Both Johnny and Billy slowly removed their bags from their backs and sat them down on the ground.

"No one comes out this way from Wakesfield. State your name and business."

"Before we do, you should know about the state of things a few hours back. You see, there are—"

"Silence!" commanded the same member of the P.A.W.

The man approached them, getting right up to their faces.

"I don't care about anything else right now other than your names and your business. Either tell me, or we're going to have a problem."

Johnny and Billy looked at one another.

"You don't want a problem now, do you, boys?"

They both shook their heads, nervously.

"Very good. Now, state your names and business."

"Sir, we were the ones who just passed the first wall—a pigeon was sent ahead that Wallace let us pass," states Johnny.

"I don't care who let you pass. State your names and business. Now! I will not tell you again!" shouted a member of P.A.W.

"My name is John Hunderson Jr., and this is my brother Billy Hunderson. We're headed out of Wakesfield to meet up with our family."

"Hunderson?"

"Yes, sir," commented Billy.

"I know that name."

Billy and Johnny stood limber.

"I am Wall Two," said the man, stepping back from the faces of Johnny and Billy, "I served with your older brother Derex. I'm sorry for your loss."

Both Johnny and Billy looked at each other then back at the member of P.A.W.

"Oh, oh my. Did you not hear?"

"Hear what?" asked Johnny and Billy.

"Your older brother Derex was sent on a special mission and his whole team was killed in the blink of an eye. Something strong wiped them all out. Derex tried to fight but ultimately ran for his life."

"Where did he die?"

"Well, we don't exactly know if he's dead, but we haven't any contact with him in a quarter since he was deployed to Dry Bone Drifts in the Sand Region."

Johnny lowered his head and shook it. A look of great loss spread across his face.

Derex.

Johnny knelt on one knee. Billy, unsure of what Johnny was doing and not wanting to stand out, followed suit. Johnny placed his hand over his upper right chest, right where his Black Dragon's foot tattoo resided. Billy copied Johnny's movement. Johnny held his hand there for a moment and whispered something inaudible. He then lifted his head and removed his right hand from his upper right chest. He rose back to his feet and looked at Wall Two. Billy did the same.

"If you want to know where my brother is, you'll find him not much farther back," said Johnny.

"You saw him?"

"Yes . . . I didn't realize it until just now, but he asked me if I had recognized him. I hadn't seen him in so long."

"Johnny, was the man to whom you were speaking Derex? The one murmuring up against the wall?" asked Billy.

"Yes, Billy. That was he."

"Murmuring? Whatever about?" asked the member of P.A.W.

"He kept going on about some approaching shadow; a darkness and how strong they are. I well imagine you know about whom he is speaking?" said Johnny.

"That I do. I'm afraid that due to limited information at this time, we're not allowed to speak about such things."

"Come on, he was my brother and your friend!"

"Trust me, Johnny, it's better that you don't know. Now, I must ask for security, what family are you going to see?"

"They're in the Bulwark Bazaar."

"Their names?"

"We're not allowed to speak about such things," said Johnny giving the P.A.W. member a deathly glare.

The P.A.W. member raised his hand then brought it down which signaled his men to lower their weapons.

"Let them pass."

"Sir? They didn't state their business fully."

"They stated it enough, Sergeant."

The P.A.W. member looked at Johnny who still eyed him with

vicious intent. The P.A.W. member nodded his head then both he and his men stepped to the side. He commanded to the P.A.W. member in the post to open the wall.

"Go on ahead, boys. Just be careful out there. I don't know what you're getting yourselves into, but with you Hunderson boys it can't be safe."

"Thanks . . ." said Johnny, swallowing hard.

Johnny and Billy went on by the P.A.W. members and exited through the second wall, and as soon as they did, it closed behind them. When it slammed shut, some dust kicked up from the cobblestone street and floated onto Johnny's tunic. He was quick to brush it off.

"One more wall to go, Billy."

"I can't believe Derex is gone."

"I can't either, but this fuels me even more," Johnny said, clenching his fist. He quickly turned around and punched the stone wall.

"Johnny, are you all right?!" asked Billy.

"I'm fine . . ."

There was a long pause before Johnny removed his hand from the wall and brushed off the dust.

"We need to keep moving, Billy. If this demon is responsible for this, we need to get to it before it wipes out anyone else, especially any more members of our family."

Could this be what Wallace was saying? The Demon of the Sand Region?

Johnny and Billy moved farther away from the Waning Wall, the second wall that put any travel to an immediate halt.

"Where does the map say we are now?" asked Billy.

Johnny pulls out the map, studying it thoroughly before responding to Billy.

"Atlas Row."

"Atlas? Like the—"

"The map. Yes. Let's go."

Johnny and Billy moved farther away from the wall and they were now on the city's outer limits and arrived closer to the final wall. While there was little left of the outer city of Wakesfield, there was, however, one of the command stations for P.A.W.

Not much farther past the outer city were the city limits. The city limits were comprised of giant citadel like stone walls; they extended for miles on end and high up into the sky. These were to ensure that those not welcomed to Wakesfield were kept out, and its residents were kept secure. Here laid another command station of P.A.W. This was one of the more forceful stations as they were the first stop for anyone who entered Wakesfield, and the last stop for anyone who exited, unless of course one exited without their knowing. It was nightfall again once Johnny and Billy arrived at the city limits. As they did, they approached another P.A.W. command station. This time, they saw triple the P.A.W. members than at the last two combined.

Chapter 8

J ohnny and Billy made their approach towards the P.A.W. command station, with light feet. Once again, they were immediately greeted by an excess of batons, all pointed at them, as well as balisongs. From the distance the brothers stood, they saw just how sharp the balisongs were.

"State your reason for departure," said an officer.

"My brother and I are off to Bulwark Bazaar to meet some relatives," replies Johnny.

"Time of return?" asked Wall Three.

"That's the thing, officer, I'm sure you have relatives and with that comes the fun of not knowing how long your time together will last. I would like to say we'll be back within a bit's time, but I can't really say. We haven't seen them in two full waves."

"Ah yes, I heard from an officer that you two would be arriving. Very well. You may exit. Enjoy the time spent with your relatives, boys."

As Wall Three reached for his key, the other members of P.A.W. slowly began to lower their weapons. As Wall Three pulled out his key, a flock of pigeons soared in, and landed on every available arm of the P.A.W.

"This can't be good," Johnny said, whispering to Billy.

Each of the P.A.W. members opened the letter from the pigeon and began reading the coded message. Almost instantly they raised their weapons back up, pointed at the Hunderson brothers.

"It's them! These are the two wanted in conjunction with the Coheod Market incident. Get them!" commanded Wall Three.

The swarm of P.A.W. members rushed at the brothers and attempted to subdue and arrest them.

"We have to get that key, Billy. It's our only chance!"

One P.A.W. member swung her baton at Johnny, and he was quick to dodge this attack, but as he did, he was shoved by another female P.A.W. member. As quickly as Johnny fell, he rose and faced off against both of the female P.A.W. members.

"Your move!" goads Johnny.

The two female members moved in, and both swung their batons. Johnny stepped backwards so both of their batons collided. He grimaced as their batons clobbered against one another, but his grimace was short lived as another P.A.W. member grabbed him from behind.

Johnny tried to shake free but could not, due to the immense strength of this female P.A.W. member. He then stepped on her foot and extended his leg back, kicked her, which knocked her back. Johnny is again approached by the two female P.A.W. members, and with their batons extended, swung at Johnny. He learned from his previous mistake of not minding his surroundings and Johnny this time grabbed both of the batons, then crossed them over one another, used his weight and pushed them down to the ground, which brought both guards down with him.

Johnny then released his grip of the batons, and as the P.A.W. members raised them back up, Johnny ducked underneath them, when they rose back up they made contact with the female P.A.W. member's face who had just previously held onto Johnny from behind.

"Billy, you good?"

Billy had three members of the P.A.W. that stared him down. They all moved in for an attack, which Billy, nicknamed the Hunderdodge, had no problem avoiding.

"A little busy here," said Billy frantically.

"The point is to subdue them; you can't do that if all you're doing is avoiding them."

"I'm well aware," responds Billy.

"Then do something! I can't fight them all by myself."

"Maybe you don't have to . . . I'll run up to the one with the key and I'll gr-"

Before Billy was able to finish his sentence, he was struck by one of the batons, right on his collar bone area, which knocked him out cold.

"Billy!"

Johnny, in a fit of rage, ran over towards Billy and shoved off the P.A.W. members. It was not long before Johnny was overwhelmed by the surmounting members of the P.A.W.

"Cease your fighting if you want to live, boy," said Wall Three.

"Never! I will not let my mission end here."

"Consider carefully what you're saying, boy. If you continue, not only will you perish, but your brother will, too. This is the last time I'm going to offer. Cease and desist. Kneel down and put your hands above your head."

Johnny stared in defeat, looked back at Billy then back at Wall Three.

This can't be it!

As Johnny was about to kneel down, another swarm of pigeons arrived. Only this time, they didn't land on the arms of the P.A.W., but instead began attacking them. As Johnny ducked for cover and crawled over toward Billy, he saw a figure that appeared from the swarm of carrier pigeons.

It can't be . . .

"Johnny, take Billy and go!"

"Wallace?"

"Johnny, go, now! The key is on that Major over there," Wallace said, motioning to Wall Three.

"What about you?"

"It's time for a change of scenery. I'll be fine. Now go! Find your father's killer and avenge him and your brother. My uncle and cousin."

Johnny snuck up to Wall Three and swept him down to his feet. He quickly grabbed the key then ducked and moved back over to Billy. He lifted him up and put him over his shoulder.

"Wallace, what was the name of the person you were trying to tell me about earlier?"

"Go! I'll catch up with you at the Bulwark Bazaar!"

Johnny nodded, and with Billy over his shoulder, he quickly, but steadily, moved towards the wall and placed the key up against it. A stone door formed from the wall and opened quickly and widely, which granted them their exit. Johnny moved through it. As soon as he was through with Billy, the door immediately slammed shut. These doors opened and shut quickly to prevent anyone who tried to stealthily and slyly slip in as someone else exited or entered.

Johnny hustled away from the door and made his way a couple

of hundred feet away from Wakesfield. He set Billy down on the ground and looked back at Wakesfield. He saw the carrier pigeons that soared around the sky, then divebombed down as one. He heard many screams which came from the P.A.W. members.

Johnny turned around and faced Billy. As he did, there was a giant, monstrous sound heard, erupting from behind the stone walls of Wakesfield. As Johnny turned to uncover this noise, he saw nothing but a dim, purple sky. The carrier pigeons were nowhere to be seen, and the screams, much like the pigeons, were no longer heard.

What was that noise? Was it the demon? I hope Wallace is okay!

Billy stirred around on the ground.

"Billy!"

"Johnny? What happened?"

"You got knocked out by a member of the P.A.W."

"Where are we?" asks Billy, looking around.

"We're on the outside of Wakesfield. We made it."

"You fought off all those officers back there?"

"No. It was the strangest thing. Wallace showed up, presumably with all the carrier pigeons as he emerged from them."

"Wallace was there? Is he all right?"

"I don't quite know, Billy. But I've no intention of going back there to find out. He said he was going to meet us, and I surely hope he does."

"We have to make sure he's all right! He's family, Johnny."

"Billy, you didn't hear that noise I just did moments ago."

"You mean that noise that sounded like a monster?"

Johnny stared at Billy in confusion.

"You *did* hear it?"

"Well, I heard something and that's what brought me back to consciousness."

"I'm glad you're all right, but we need to keep moving. Are you okay to walk?"

"Yeah, I'm fine."

"Good, let's go then, Billy. We're headed south towards the Bulwark Bazaar Inn."

Billy looked back towards Wakesfield. His laid his eyes upon the city's lights as they gleamed against the moon and the purple sky. The giant clock tower's sound had grown quieter as the Hunderson brothers continued their adventure towards the Bulwark Bazaar. With each step taken, they got closer to finding out who killed their father.

 *Chapter 9*

J ohnny and Billy have walked for hours now, with no sight of the Bulwark Bazaar.

"How far away is this place, Johnny?"

"I'm not too sure. This map doesn't exactly give any time specifications. Almost as if you get there when you get there . . ."

"Johnny."

"Yes, Billy?"

"What if . . . What's going to happen?"

"What do you mean?" asked Johnny.

"With this adventure. Are we returning home?"

"I don't know, Billy."

"And why're we going south? Why not head west? There's an entrance to the Forest Region that's closer, is there not?"

"How do you know that?"

"The map. When you were sleeping one night back before we found the Warning Wall, I was looking at the map."

"Why?"

"I'm inquisitive, what can I say?"

They both continued walking on and as the moon faded, then sun rose.

"Johnny, can we rest? We've been walking all night."

"I don't want to stop and rest in the morning . . . We're in dangerous new terrain here, Billy. We have no idea what is out here. We need to st—"

"Stay focused, I got it."

"Are you sure?" asked Johnny, "Last I saw, you weren't focused and took a baton that knocked you out cold.

They both laughed, although Johnny was less amused than Billy. They continued their journey, walked all throughout the day, snacked on their food, and drank their water to satiate them. As another day passed and turned into night, the moon shined in the sky above once more.

"We shall rest here for the night, Billy."

"Great!"

They both set up their respective areas and laid down for the night, and drifted off quickly into a deep sleep, which allowed their body the time it needed to recover from the battle in which they were entangled. As the moon faded, so too did the dreams of Johnny and Billy, and the sun rose once more.

"Let's get moving," said Johnny, rising to his feet.

Both he and Billy gathered up all their items and continued making their way toward Bulwark Bazaar.

"What does the map say about the bazaar, Johnny?"

"Not much. Just really said it's a main hub for information. It's either incredibly big, or incredibly small."

"Why do you say that?"

"Well, there seem to be multiple parts to it, but I can't seem to make it out; maybe they're smudge marks or actual parts."

"I suppose we'll find out soon enough, huh?" asked Billy.

"Yes. A bazaar where strangers share their wealth of information."

As the Hunderson brothers continued walking, the sun above them began to fade, but not due to the time of day. Instead, a giant object began to obscure it, getting larger the closer they got.

"I think we just found our answer, Billy."

Before both Johnny and Billy was the Bulwark Bazaar, which stood tall with its ship-shaped building.

"It looks like there are different tiers to the building, Billy."

"It would seem so, but it's so large it's difficult to tell!"

As they got even closer, the sun was completely blocked out from the Bulwark Bazaar, much like an eclipse taking over.

As they approached the entrance, they saw many different wanderers that strutted about the front and headed down the sides of the building, into the varying entrances and alleys.

"Let us head inside, Billy, but keep your wits about you. We know nothing of these people and there isn't exactly a police force like in Wakesfield to protect us."

Johnny and Billy entered the Bulwark Bazaar and the first thing they saw was a wooden desk, surrounded by a wooden floor, with a few plants scattered around either side of the desk.

"Hello, sirs, what may we do for you today?" asked the innkeeper at the front desk.

"Yes, keeper, my brother and I are in need of some information," replied Johnny.

"And what information might that be, sir?"

"Well, we're looking for a demon, you see. Has anyone by the name Demon of the Sand Region passed through here lately?"

"I'm sorry, sir, but I don't think I'm the right person to be asking this. I'll be happy to assist you in finding a comfort station."

"Which we will come back to you later for, but right now, we need information."

Both Johnny and the Keeper stared at one another in a sort of deadlock.

"Comfort station before information, that's our motto!"

"I'm sure it is," replied Johnny with a grimace, "Two comfort stations then, keeper."

"Very well. Follow me this way to your stations."

The Keeper led Johnny and Billy through the main area of the bazaar, which consisted of a giant open eating area, with wooden tables and chairs, as well as a bar.

"The workers here are so well-dressed," said Billy to Johnny.

"Everything seems to be perfect," replied Johnny.

"Almost too perfect."

The three of them reached the comfort stations which were nothing more than a wooden bed with a heaping pile of hay sprawled out across the surface.

"Comfort huh?" asked Billy sarcastically.

"Yes, sir, we have had to make many additions to the bazaar due to the influx of the wanderers who have lost their homes to the war. Please bear with us as we continue to improve. Thank you!" replied the Keeper with a false cheeriness.

"Okay, we've seen our comfort stations. Now, about the information?" asked Johnny.

"Yes, sir, let me just record down your names and book them in our register, give you your membership cards, then you will be free to roam about and enjoy your stay."

"Membership cards?" asked Billy.

"Oh yes, anyone who passes through the Bulwark Bazaar is granted a membership card, allowing them access."

"Do they expire? I mean, what's to stop someone from coming back in a bit or a half and trying to use a comfort station?" asked Johnny.

"We have our way we keep everything monitored, not to worry, sir," replied the Keeper.

"Right, well, take down our names so we may be on our way," said Johnny.

"Oh I already know who you sirs are. Mr. Thomas speaks very highly of you both. He has known your family for many waves."

"Thomas, eh?" asked Johnny.

"Yes. And there you go, all logged in. Here are your membership cards. Dinner time will be upon us soon and we will be dimming the lights here in the main dining hall to reflect this. Don't be alarmed. Enjoy your stay, sirs!"

"Thank you, keeper," replied both Johnny and Billy.

As the Keeper returned to his post, back through the dining room, he relieved the man who took his place, and this man went outside.

"They have this place on some weird kind of tightly wound schtick."

"What do you mean, Johnny?" asked Billy.

"It's as if they're military or something. I mean come on, the way they have everything so perfect here, the constant watch . . . Look over your left shoulder, Billy, seven o'clock."

Billy complied and discreetly looked over his shoulder. When he did, he saw a man dressed in all black seated at a table in the corner. The upper half of this man was cloaked in shadow due to the dimness of the lighting due to the dinner setting for the lights.

"We're being watched right now. What do you say we start with him, first?"

"Johnny, don't do anything to get us in trouble," said Billy in a worried tone.

"Come now, Billy, we'll be fine. Your big brother will protect you," said Johnny with glee.

They approached the man who had stared at them.

"May we sit down?" asked Johnny.

"Please," replied the man, motioning to the chairs.

"Couldn't help but notice you were looking at us."

"Yes, I had overheard your conversation on the way in," replied the man.

"The entrance is something like fifty feet away from here. How did you hear anything?" asked Johnny.

A smirk appeared on the man's face.

"You didn't know if it was us or another person. You just wanted to confirm, and I just did that for you. What do you want?" asked Johnny.

"I take it you're Johnny. The direct approach, fearless, engaging," said the man, scanning Johnny up and down before shifting his eyes to Billy. "And you. Shy, timid, skittish. You must be his younger brother Billy."

"Excuse me there for a moment. I'm not saying I disagree with your assessment of my brother, but do not insult my family again," Johnny said sternly.

"Don't get all riled up now. We're both seeking the same thing. A demon."

Johnny raised an eyebrow.

"What exactly do you know?" asked Johnny.

They both stared at one another.

"As a matter of fact, what's your name?" asked Johnny.

"No need for names. Do you want the information or not?"

"What I want is for the both of us to step outside so we may handle this more accordingly, but I don't think you want that," said Johnny.

"You threatening me, boy?"

"No. Merely making an observation. You think you're so sly, but from the moment we walked by you were eyeing the both of us. After that, you quickly looked around to see if there was anyone else around. You need something from us, but you're also hiding from someone and you don't wish to arouse suspicion."

"Very astute, Mr. Hunderson. You truly are as clever as they say."

"Depends on who *they* are," replied Johnny.

The two continued to keep their eyes locked on one another, as if they were both in some intense chess match, waiting for their opponent to make a mistake and give them the upper hand.

"That's twice now I've heard that and, I'll admit, my curiosity is piqued, but that's not why I'm here," said Johnny.

"As if you'd be able to handle it anyway," said the man as he let out a small chuckle.

"What are you two talking about?" Billy chimed in.

"Ask your brother here. After all, Derex told him all about it."

Johnny slid his chair back and quickly reached across the table, grabbed the man by his collar with one hand and pulled him closer so he was under the light. As he did, he saw this man was wearing a mask.

"Easy now, Mr. Hunderson. You don't want to attract the wrong attention."

"I don't think you have the slightest idea of what I want. This is twice now you've mentioned something about my family. There will not be a third," replied Johnny aggressively.

The man grabbed Johnny's hand and squeezed it, tightly.

"First of all, that is an empty threat. You are less than a gnat to me. Second, this isn't Wakesfield. You know nothing about anything beyond the Stone City. You don't even know what demon you're after."

Johnny threw a punch with his other hand, but the man was quick to smack it down and gripped Johnny's hand tighter. He then pulled him across the table and shoved him against the bar, shattering some glasses, then grabbed him once more and shoved him to the floor.

"Johnny!"

Billy quickly rose.

"Don't bother, boy. You're no match for me, nor is your brother. Both of you are about to enter something bigger than you understand."

"Is that why you wear a mask?" asked Johnny, slowly rising to his feet, "Afraid of someone spotting you? Maybe even recognizing you, Ryan."

The man's eyes widened and glowed in bewilderment. He stood up from the table.

"Ryan?" questioned Billy.

"Yes, Billy. I'd like you to meet another brother of yours. A disgrace to our family name . . . Ryan Hunderson."

 *Chapter 10*

Johnny stared at the man as he rose back up to his feet. He brushed himself off.

"How did you know?" asks Ryan.

"You have the same snarky, condescending tone from our childhood. That, and look down at your tunic."

Ryan looked down and saw it was ruffled and ripped a little bit in the upper right chest area.

"You're not as astute as you used to be, but I ripped off a little bit of your tunic the moment you grabbed my hand."

"You had a feeling it was me but didn't know until you saw my stupid Black Dragon's foot tattoo," replies Ryan.

"What's going on here?" asks Billy.

"Billy, this is Ryan. While there is a four-wave gap between you, you never met him. He ran away when you were really young. You really hurt dad, and I have a good reason to really hurt you," said Johnny.

"Are you really looking to take me on, Johnny? Remember, dad was able to make me a master of the way of the Black Dragon, unlike your pitiful self."

Johnny stepped closer to Ryan.

"Johnny, don't!" shouted Billy.

"He's right, Johnny. Not only will you lose, but it would appear we've caused quite a scene."

Johnny took a look around at the patrons who have filled the room for dinner and noticed the employees that moved in slowly.

"What do you say the three of us take this conversation elsewhere?"

"You have somewhere in mind, Ryan?" asks Johnny.

"Yes, follow me."

The three of them exited the main dining hall and made their way down a hallway, up a set of stairs and onto a different section of the bazaar.

"An open roof area, I suppose we were right, Billy."

"Yes, that map of yours seems to be coming in handy."

Johnny paused for a moment before he came to a realization.

"It was you that day in Wakesfield. You tapped me on the shoulder. You asked me for the time. You told me about the Forest Region."

"Yes, Johnny," replied Ryan.

"How did you get in? You ran away, mom and dad told us you left the city. That's no easy feat."

"There are other ways to enter Wakesfield than the walls."

"There are?" asked Johnny.

"This is exactly what I mean, you're so inexperienced it's laughable!"

"Said the one who disgraced our family," replied Johnny.

"Johnny, the fact that you didn't even recognize my face when you saw me goes to show that you can't even recognize the truth," said Ryan, removing his mask.

Johnny took a moment.

"When you asked me for the time the other day, you had a scar on your face. It looked like a bad burn mark."

"Yes, I, well, I ran into some trouble. This is why I put on the mask."

"Ryan, what is going on? I'm furious with you but the more you speak the more my interest becomes piqued as to just what is really going on."

"Then grab a seat and allow me to explain a few things."

Both Johnny and Billy sat down.

"You probably remember mom telling you how I ran away and how it broke dad's heart. How he saw me as a failure, as a disgrace to the family, right?"

"Well yeah, but-"

"Did you ever ask dad about me?"

Johnny sat speechless.

"That's what I thought. Mom fed you lies about me and blamed it on dad. She knew that you wouldn't understand the truth and that, even if she told you, you wouldn't believe it anyway."

"What truth?" asked Johnny.

"The final test," said Ryan firmly, adjusting his tunic.

"Final test?"

"Yes, the final test. The thing needed to be done to become a true master in the way of the Black Dragon and the Lion, respectively."

"There's a final test for me, too?" asks Billy.

"Yes, but it's not like any test we've taken before. It's . . . it's maddening. The very thought of it drove our own mother to insanity."

"What happened to her?" asks Johnny.

"She's entranced in the Twilight Region."

"The Twilight Region?"

"Pull out the map," barked Ryan.

Johnny complied and pulled out the map from his bag, opened it up and held it for Ryan.

"This here, this is the Twilight Region," Ryan spoke, jabbing a finger at the map.

"That tiny pink dot on the map?" asked Johnny.

"It only looks so tiny due to the enormous size of the Forest Region. However, that region is unlike the others—there's nothing there. At least not when I last went there."

"Then why the pink dot?" asked Johnny, scratching his head.

"That's the general location of it, but that pink dot represents the Twilight Region. It's a region full of crepuscular pink plumes of smoke."

"Crepuscular, as in relating to twilight?" asked Billy.

"Yes, the same. That's where the region gets its name. Now, please, no more interruptions," Ryan said sternly.

Johnny and Billy nodded.

"Mom left for the Twilight Region when dad left. You see, up until recently, the Twilight Region didn't exist . . . Many things in Direfell only came to be within the past four or five waves. The day you received your tattoo is the day everything changed for the worse."

Johnny went to open his mouth to speak but paused, which allowed for Ryan to have an uninterrupted speech.

"That is the day your final test began, unbeknownst to you. However, yours is different. The final test wasn't supposed to be anything like this—there wasn't a war going on when I had mine and they weren't coming back."

"Who are *they?* We keep talking about it with no end in sight. Can we use a different pronoun at least? I know you said not to interrupt but you're telling us so much. I have so many questions!"

"I understand this is a lot, trust me I do. And I know you may even be questioning on whether or not to believe me after what you've been told about me. There are a far great deal of things in Direfell that have changed and I'm telling you this because it all has to do with you. Have you ever heard the story of the Clayappose?"

"No, I haven't," responds Johnny.

"Nor have I," replies Billy.

"The Clayappose is looking for you, Johnny, and they are going to find you. It's not a matter of if, but when . . . When they do, I don't know what's going to happen. I've read up about this situation. I don't know if it's true or not, but something about you attracted the Clayappose's attention. Last I heard, the Clayappose is in the Forest Region and this is where you need to go."

"That's where we're trying to get. We're looking for a demon. Wallace was trying to tell me, but I didn't catch all of it."

Johnny noticed a slight tremor cross Ryan's hands.

"What's wrong?" asks Johnny.

"Stay away from Wallace, okay, Johnny? Billy?"

"Why?" both Johnny and Billy ask.

"There are many foul things out there in Direfell, some of which are too strong and powerful for even me to handle . . . Nevertheless, if you see him, run!"

"Ryan, what is going on? You're turning our whole idea of family upside right now, how do I know if I should even believe you?"

"You're smart enough to know that when there's one telling an impossible truth within a sea of uncertainty that that's the real truth."

"Even if I am smart enough to realize that, it still doesn't make sense."

"Johnny said Wallace saved us from the P.A.W." said Billy.

"*Saved you* or spared you?" asked Ryan, in a chilling tone.

Johnny and Billy sat completely still, absolutely stunned by Ryan's accusation.

"I don't know what his mission is, but I'll tell you it is not in align with yours."

"What is this all about?"

"There's a lot you need to know, Johnny, but the more I tell you the more questions it will beg . . . Let me leave you with this. The demon for whom you're looking is the Demon of the North. It resides on the North End of the Forest Region."

"The Demon of the North? That's who Wallace was trying to tell me about," replied Johnny.

"Oh I'm sure he was, it'd be all too fitting," replied Ryan.

"What do you mean?" asked Johnny.

"Didn't it ever strike you odd that Wallace's last name is different from ours?"

"No. Why should it, he's our cousin and cousins can have different last names."

"True, but that's if our father had a sister who got married," replies Ryan.

"I only know about Uncle Dumont, I never got to meet the rest of our family, if we even have any."

Ryan lingered in his speech, shocked by Johnny's statement.

"It's amazing how little you know, Johnny. The reason that Wallace-" Ryan shifted his attention to a staff member who had just arrived on the roof.

"We're having a private conversation here, do you mind?" asked Ryan.

"Private conversations should be kept private. You never know who might be listening," replied the staff member.

Ryan fully turned around and spoke to the staff member. As he did, his eyes widened, and his hand shook once more. He turned his head slightly to Johnny and Billy.

"That will be all now, gentlemen. Thank you!"

"What? Ryan what-"

"That will be all, I said. I'll meet you two back downstairs in the main dining hall. Order me a pid of what's on tap."

"Sure thing!" replied Johnny, quickly grabbing Billy and hurriedly getting off the open roof area, heading back down another set of stairs and back down to the main dining room.

"Johnny, what's going on? What's a pid?"

"For as little time as Ryan and I got to spend together, we grew close, much like you and I are. After all, he's only two waves older than I am, much like how I'm two waves older than you."

"I don't understand," replied Billy.

"We grew close for one scouting trip that we went on by ourselves. The first and only scouting trip we went on without dad. We wanted to have a code word in case either of us got in trouble. You see, a pid is like a mug or a pint. Essentially something for you to put your drink in. However, they haven't been in circulation for quite some time now, as most bars have moved on to more up-to-date things like pints and mugs."

"I'm still not getting this; pid is a code word?"

"Yes, Billy. It means *Potentially In Danger*. Ryan was warning us to evacuate the roof because whomever he saw up there wasn't a staff member."

"What? Who was it then?" asked Billy.

"I'm not sure, but whoever it was putting him on edge. I have never seen Ryan shake like that. He's much better than I am in every aspect of fighting," said Johnny.

"Much like you are with me, huh Johnny?"

"Your words, Billy."

"Oh come on. I see how you look at me, I know it's true. I know you're better than me, but I'll get there eventually!"

"You will, and I'll make sure of that, but for now, we need to get a different comfort station. One near the back of this place."

The two of them moved down the corridor and through the main dining hall and back to the front desk.

"Keeper, hello, my brother and I would like a different comfort station if we may."

"Sure thing, sirs, I just need to ask a few routine questions."

"No problem, let's walk and talk," said Johnny.

The three of them moved to another part of the bazaar, this time heading down the corridor behind the wooden desk at the main front entrance.

"Discomfort?" asked the keeper.

"Something like that," said Johnny.

"Any particular area in the back section, gentlemen?"

"Yes, somewhere close to the South End of the Forest Region. We'd like to get an early start there. Is there a direct path we may take?"

"Yes, I know just the spot! In fact, there's a bridge that will lead you there directly. Once you cross it, you'll be in the South End of Direfell, and not far from there you'll find the South End of the Forest Region."

"Thank you, keeper," said Johnny.

"Although I don't know why anyone would want to go into that place."

"My brother and I want to explore all the regions. We have a sort of bucket list."

"Ah yes, sir, not my place to question your reasons. Merely just my opinion. I shall mind my tongue."

"Not a problem at all, keeper."

"Very good, sir. We're almost to the back area here."

"And from here, how far is the journey to the bridge?" asked Johnny.

"With speed like yours, it will be a three-day journey."

Speed like ours?" asked Johnny.

"Yes, sir, it's just a common expression."

"Not so common to me, I've never heard of it," Johnny replied.

"Fair enough, sir. Here we are. If you are hungry, ring the bell and we will have one of our employees bring you some options for food. Or, if you like, visit one of our many dining halls."

"Thank you, keeper."

Both Johnny and Billy stared at the comfort station. Theirs was in the style of a bunkbed; one station on top of the other. They're lucky to have found, or have gotten, two stations in the same area. The brothers had quickly learned that Bulwark Bazaar was a vast place with many corridors to visit.

It was teemed with people who lived here due to losing their homes from the previous wars, and the subtle war that exists. This war was subtle because not much is known about it . . . There was an effort being made by all parties to claim land and to have one rule govern over all. This war was not as great as the previous wars but had the potential to turn into the biggest war Direfell had ever seen!

This was why many sought refuge and safety in the Bulwark Bazaar Inn—the corridors led to many different comfort stations. These different comfort stations were in a better area of the land as some areas in which the comfort stations are designated had tree branches that poked out from them, or a pile of leaves, scattered all over the bed.

This was due to the one end of Bulwark Bazaar being so close to the Forest Region. This was the area in which both Johnny and Billy chose as they wanted to make haste to the Forest Region in the early morning. Their particular comfort station had a tree branch poking through the top station, while the bottom one had leaves everywhere, covering the floor and the station itself.

"Here you are, gentlemen. Have a good night," said the keeper.

"How? I have a tree branch poking through where I'm supposed to be sleeping," commented Billy.

"We have a full disclosure sign up front-"

"It's fine, thank you. He was just joking around," said Johnny.

Billy gave Johnny a look.

"Rest up, Billy. We're leaving early in the morning," said Johnny.

"What about Ryan, Johnny?"

"Shh!" said Johnny, "I don't want to attract any attention to us back here. I don't know what's going to happen with him, but I do know he can take care of himself. Don't worry, Billy!"

Amidst my telling Billy not to worry about Ryan, I can't help to think about everything he told me and worry even more. I've never seen him like that, but it happened when I mentioned Wallace. What is going on?

"Johnny?"

"Yes, Billy."

"Do we really have to leave first thing in the morning?"

"Yes, Billy. Whoever that was that found our brother, I don't want them finding us."

Is it the demon Ryan was telling me about? This thing is really starting to peeve me. First my father, then Derex, now Ryan. Or was it the Clayappose? Either way, I need to face this Demon of the North alone. I can't risk Billy coming to the same fate as the others. Maybe facing this demon is the final test Ryan was talking about.

The leaves on the floor began to rustle as the brothers set down their bags and got into their respective beds. Billy gave his best attempt to get comfortable in his station. Part of the tree branch forced its way out of the wooden station. Billy's feet brushed up against the dark, hard bark. He pulled his legs closer to him almost in the position in which an infant would sleep so that he may get some rest.

Johnny, on the other hand, had no problem with his comfort station—he was used to sleeping in less comfortable sleeping situations due to his many scouting trips with his father and the one with his brother Ryan. He fell right into the station, the leaves rustled under his body with every movement, which welcomed him almost in a comforting way. Johnny drifted off and for once, he fell asleep. He didn't get up and leave Billy to go off and roam through the night.

Nevertheless, as soon as morning arrived, his eyes peered open and he rose from his comfort station, with the leaves clung to his shoulders and back as he sat up.

# Chapter 11

Johnny got out of the comfort station and gathered up all of his gear. He took in his surroundings and surveyed if there were any others around. He then looked to Billy.

"Billy. Let's move," ordered Johnny.

Billy stirred in his comfort station. He yawned, opened his eyes and rubbed them.

"You weren't kidding; first thing, eh?" asked Billy sarcastically.

"Now," demanded Johnny.

"Johnny, why're you so rude to me? You were telling Ryan how he has a condescending tone, well you do, too!"

"Billy—"

"Billy nothing! You could try saying things in a nicer tone, you know."

"And you could try not getting so offended by words. If you allow words to affect you, Billy, then anyone can control you . . . Just relax. I'll try to be less demanding, but it's just in my nature."

"And?"

"And what?"

"How about an apology?" Billy said sternly.

"I'm sorry . . . you think you're getting an apology," said Johnny, jokingly, patting Billy on the shoulder.

The two of them packed up their things and made their way

toward the door farther down the hall from them. As they both exited, they looked up at the barely lit sky. The two of them made their travel toward the Forest Region.

"Based off what the keeper said, we'll be taking this path leading south," said Johnny.

They travelled along a dirt trail accompanied by grass on either side, that led farther south, away from the Bulwark Bazaar Inn. Not that green, flourishing grass though, this grass was losing its green color and slowly diminishing into brown. This was due to all the dirt that had been kicked up and landed on the grass over the waves that passed.

"This is some odd-looking grass. It reminds me of the orchard back in Wakesfield," said Billy.

Initially, this area was all grass, and all the grass led straight to the Forest Region. It was difficult to navigate at first, because there was no set path to follow, but now that many travelers have made way to the South End, there was now a more defined path to take. This was not the only thing to have happened to the land. Over the passing waves, there had been many man-made things, such as secret tunnels which led to far off lands and secret bases in which secret organizations met. As to if there was any credibility to these aforementioned items, as well as the actuality of them, was yet to be determined.

"I still can't get over what was said back there," said Johnny.

"Me neither, Johnny. To think that what we've been told our whole lives has been a lie."

"Ryan was so shaken up by the mere mention of Wallace. And I can't shake the words that he didn't just let us go . . . he *spared* us."

"There are a lot of unexplained things, Johnny."

"I need explanations to these unexplained things. Most importantly of all is who killed our father. I believe there are other forces out there, but I don't even know where *there* is."

Billy nodded in agreement.

"I'm sure there are other forces out there, I just don't know which force is the darkest, or just how mysterious they are. Or even where they are, to boot!"

"How far away is this place?" asked Billy.

"Far enough away that we'll be able to tell if we're being followed. There is a scarcity to people out here the farther from the Bulwark Bazaar we get."

As the sun continued to rise in the sky, Billy and Johnny walked side by side, but Johnny stepped up his pace and took the lead. The two of them continued to travel down the dirt trail for three days, only taking short breaks here and there, and as they did they saw areas of green grass, which covered all of the land, instead of the dirty patchy ones.

"This is such a sight to see, compared to what we were just dealing with a little while back!" said Johnny, almost skipping in excitement.

Eventually, they saw more flourishing grass that led up to a forest. There stood exceptionally large, tall trees. Johnny walked up to one of the trees and ran his hand along it.

"Interesting to say the least . . ."

Johnny brushed off the pieces of bark from his hands. The trees' bark was of a dark brown color and appeared to be very old and chipped away. The trees here on the South End of were possibly created first, considering how they looked. One could never be too sure, as there was more to the history of something besides its age.

Billy looked up toward the sky and took in the sight of the enormous trees ahead of them. He then called to Johnny, who was a few steps ahead of him.

"It has to be up here somewhere, but where would this be? The keeper simply said—"

"Johnny, it's been about two hours now. Do you see the path leading toward the Forest Region or not?"

Johnny halted in his tracks and a face of disgust took over. He looked back toward Billy.

"What?" asked Billy.

"The pathway, the one that leads directly to the Forest Region is gone. Destroyed!

Billy jogged up to Johnny and took in the sight that Johnny saw.

"I don't believe it," said Johnny.

Spread far and wide before both Johnny and Billy there was a gaping hole in the land. From where they're standing, a gap was beneath them . . . There was bedrock at the base of this destruction, as well as water. This gap stretched on for quite a bit and, although the other side can be seen, it is totally inaccessible to both Johnny and Billy. Johnny took one step closer and examined the damage. It was if Johnny and Billy were standing atop a cliff and stared at the other side with no bridge to get across. The water was flowing downward and appeared to be quite deep. It gently pushed up against the bedrock and the side of the gap but didn't push up high enough to have splashed Johnny and Billy.

"This damage is fresh. There is something odd about this though . . . Who could do such a thing? To do something like this would take an immense amount of power. Power that can't . . . possibly exist," said Johnny, "I remember reading in dad's journal about these things called tactics and how people were able to learn them and shoot fire from their hands, as well as other things like ice or lightning."

"You think a person did this?" asked Billy, in a skittish tone.

"It's very well possible!"

This chasm expands far to the left heading toward the water and we're ill-equipped to traverse those uneven waves. And it looks to be to the right that the chasm seems to be never ending. Gah, we can't waste time seeing how far it goes.

Having looked a bit farther ahead, past the gap, Johnny saw a bridge. This bridge was built across something that Johnny could not make out. Another gap potentially. This bridge was old and had been there for many waves; its being was covered in vines and blades of grass. This bridge was most likely built by a traveler from long ago; someone who was on a mission to the South End and aimed for its many mysteries offered. Johnny examined the damage closer.

"This wasn't like this. Someone did this."

Why would someone want to make this area look like the one up ahead, but without a bridge? To discourage travel to the South End of Direfell? What's down there? This is indeed something to look into further . . . If I'm to just take one more step down there maybe I—

"What're we going to do?" asked Billy.

Johnny, startled by his brother's interference of his deep thought, turned to him and responded.

"We're going to have to go around the other way, back through the Bulwark Bazaar and make leave from the front entrance and reach the outskirts of the Forest Region that way."

"Fantastic! Pelf well spent on a comfort station only to have to go back through that place," remarked Billy.

"Forget about the pelf, all right? We're going back right now. I want to make it back there; we've already wasted enough time coming this way. Look, we've been travelling for three days, just like the keeper said we would be."

"He said we would take three days with our speed," replied Billy.

"I guess somehow he knew we wouldn't be stopping to rest."

"We need to rest, Johnny! That's another three day journey to go back."

"Billy, with everything that's going on, we need answers now more than ever."

"Focus."

"What?" asked Johnny.

"You're losing your focus, Johnny."

Johnny glanced at Billy in shock.

"We need to rest."

"Agreed, Billy. We'll rest for the night and first—"

"Yes, I know. First thing in the morning."

"I guess I mentioned this before, huh?"

They both shared a hearty laugh as they setup to rest for the night. As they laid down, Billy fell asleep quickly, while Johnny didn't. His body stirred much like the thoughts in his mind.

Could this be the evil force Derex was talking about, the approaching shadow? What is going on in Direfell? Everything outside of the city is just quiet, like there is no one else around—no other inhabitants of this world besides Wakesfield and the Bulwark Bazaar Inn. That can't be possible, though . . . There's the Demon of the North out there in the Forest Region.

Johnny finally lulled off to sleep just as the sun began to rise. As he did, Billy woke up, looked over at Johnny and realized he was still asleep.

"I should let him rest."

Billy glanced back to the sky and watched the clouds as they moved across the sky, slowly. Both of them got a much-deserved slumber after their three days of travel. By the time Johnny woke up, it was mid-afternoon.

"Billy, it looks like we overslept."

"It's called sleeping in, Johnny, and we needed it."

"Semantics. Let's move."

"There's that condescending tone again," said Billy.

Johnny rolled his eyes as they gathered their gear. The two of them headed back toward the Bulwark Bazaar and left the destroyed pathway in the distance.

I still can't shake where that gap came from, but no matter. Now we must find another way into the Forest Region, and I hope there is one.

Many wonders, creatures, and beings await anyone foolish enough to brave the depths of the Forest Region. It was said that those who travelled into the forest never came back out. It's not the statement or rumor that should have one startled . . . No. Instead, it should be the thought of decision or death. In other words, did those who have never returned from the Forest Region do this on their own accord, or was it due to them succumbing to their untimely end? There were many wonders to be discovered in the entirety of the land, but for this particular adventure . . . the forest is beckoning to the Hundersons.

Billy trotted toward Johnny and began walking next to him.

"Johnny, I know it's kind of an odd time to ask, but while we're heading back to the inn, I was wondering . . . Well, I was wondering why you never enlisted?"

"Enlisted? Well, I didn't want to be just another Hunderson boy throwing his life away to the war," said Johnny.

"It was the letter, wasn't it?"

"Look, my life is relatively peaceful in the respect that I'm not fighting in a war right now."

"You're about to enter one, are you not? Barging into the Forest Region not knowing about anything that's out there, or rather, in there," replied Billy.

"I suppose you're right in one regard, Billy. I will enter in there with little to no knowledge of the area. A map would surely come in handy, but no local store seems to sell them, and the one I have from dad's room doesn't do us any good. It's just a giant area with nothing marked besides the different ends. I imagine this is due to no one ever returning from the Forest Region."

"And what about starting a war? I mean if this demon is out there and as dangerous as Ryan was telling us then—"

"Then nothing. I will fight whoever I must to get whatever answers I need from this demon."

"I'm not too sure. I wish we had help . . . Someone more than just the two of us."

Johnny reflected on Billy's comment before answering.

There is no one else. I wish we could find people, especially now knowing about the things Ryan told me. The Clayappose, even having to be concerned about my own cousin Wallace.

"Enough of this talk. I don't want to hear another word while we're in the inn. I don't want the patrons knowing about our business."

"In the inn, that's pretty funny don't you think?" asked Billy.

Johnny rolled his eyes at Billy's attempted humor. Johnny and Billy approached the Bulwark Bazaar Inn. Once they reached the inn, the sky was lit, and the morning sun ascended. They made their way back toward the front of the building and Johnny had a word with the inn keeper.

"Hey, buddy!"

"Yes, sir?" said the Keeper, cowardly.

"Why didn't you tell me the pathway to the Forest Region was destroyed?" asked Johnny.

"You didn't ask, sir."

"Listen, smart mouth, you knew that's why I requested that side," replied Johnny.

"I've no idea what you're on about, sir."

"This is ridiculous, keeper!" Johnny said, slamming his fist down on the front desk.

"I don't understand why you're getting so mad, sir. Just leave and make your way toward the Forest Region from your home city."

"What was the point of even telling me about the other way then?"

"Sir, when I told you about it, that pathway was intact. As for who destroyed it? That is far beyond my knowledge."

Johnny glared intently at the Inn Keeper.

The pathway was still intact? This means that it was a pathway. Then why would someone destroy it? Is someone onto us? Could some-one have possibly overheard my plans to go to the Forest Region?

"Hey, uh, Johnny. There are some mean looking fellows coming our way," stated Billy.

"Come on, Billy, we're leaving."

"Hey, you. Mr. Rough-Em-Up."

Johnny ceased walking. He turned around and saw a stocky man stood a few feet before him. This man rolled up his sleeves and stared down Johnny.

"Yeah, I'm talking to you, you black tunic wearing, red bandana wearing piece of detritus. You got some real nerve coming up in here causing a ruckus in our place of establishment," said a boisterous employee.

"In your place of establishment? Do you own this place?" asked Johnny, "Funny, you don't look like Thomas."

"What's it to you?"

"Well," said Johnny, "Seeing as you approached me in such an upset manner, I suppose you would like something to be done about all of this? That some form of payment be made to you?"

"Yeah, that sounds about right."

"I don't have pelf to pay."

"That's just fine . . . We didn't really want pelf anyway. You wrecked our dining hall from that scene you caused about a bit ago. And now we're going to wreck you."

"Johnny, come on, let's get out of here!" said Billy.

"And what? Have them follow us?"

"We can report them to the P.A.W.," said Billy.

"You're joking, right? We can't go back there. Plus, unless we're in the city limits, it's out of their jurisdiction."

"Hey. You done talking over there or what?"

"Yeah. I'm done talking. Come at me."

The man who previously spoke to Johnny ran at him. Johnny, let a smirk crack over his face, then stepped to the side and tripped him.

"Amateur," Johnny said, scoffing.

"I'll teach you!"

The man got up, formed a fist and turned once more and threw the punch at Johnny.

"If you keep using those same moves, you'll never lay a hand on me," said Johnny.

"You think?"

"All the time, you should try it!" said Johnny, letting another smile cross his face.

"You think you're so tough, huh?"

"You're about to find out!"

The man threw another punch, and Johnny once more stepped to the side, this time he turned slightly, pushed the man, used his force from this punch and pushed him further. The man caught himself, turned to face Johnny, and got knocked right in the face, he stumbled back.

"I'm on a bit of a time crunch. Is there anyone else who doesn't want pelf, but wants a piece of me instead? No? Didn't think so."

Billy, dumbfounded, looked at the inn keeper, who was fixed on Johnny, who was headed for the door.

"Come on, Billy. We're leaving."

Johnny and Billy made their way out of the Bulwark Bazaar and left beaten men and a dumbfounded inn keeper.

That was pathetic. Some of these people have no training, no skills to speak of. It's laughable.

On their way out of the Bulwark Bazaar, Billy looked up to the sky and saw a flock of birds that soared over them. He smiled.

"Robins."

"Did you say something, Billy?"

"Yeah, there are robins flying above us."

Johnny looked up to the sky and saw the robins about which Billy spoke.

"We're not going back home to restock, are we?" asked Billy.

"We can't, Billy. The P.A.W. is still looking for us. We'll have to use our training we got from the scouting trips and scavenge food along the way."

"We should've packed more food," said Billy.

"I wasn't expecting this to take as long as it is. We got plenty of food from the bazaar and that should last us until we get to the Forest Region."

"What about finding a way in? What are we going to do?"

"There must be something I'm missing on this map. The south can't be the only entrance into the Forest Region," said Johnny.

They continued on and made their way back in the direction of Wakesfield. From there, they would find another path leading to the Forest Region. This path they headed toward led them to another part of the land, far away from the Bulwark Bazaar and far away from the South End.

"Once we make it back to the far outskirts of Wakesfield, we'll rest there."

"Sounds good to me, Johnny."

After having walked for two days, the brothers reached the outskirts of Wakesfield, making sure they stayed far enough away from it to avoid any P.A.W. members who patrolled. As they continued walking, they saw a post with different wooden signs on them.

"Let's read up on these signs and see if it gives a distance from here to the Forest Region," said Johnny.

Billy took in all the Stone City had to offer from its glorious outside view. A smile lit up his face for a moment, only for it to fade away as he turned left and continued down a dirt trail, which led him farther and farther away from Wakesfield. As they continued down the path, the Stone City became smaller and smaller, and soon dwindled away into nothing more than a small sight upon which to be gazed as it slowly became nothing more than a thought, deep into the night.

"You didn't even look."

"Look at what?" asked Johnny.

"At our home!"

"What's there to see? It's a giant city made of stone," said Johnny.

"Even so, you don't know when or if we'll be returning to this place. We're off on some adventure—"

"An adventure about which you were excited."

"Yes, until I realized just what kind of adventure this actually was," replied Billy.

"And what would that be?" asked Johnny.

"A suicide mission! You don't know who this man is, what he does, or anything about the Forest Region. All you have is an idea planted in your mind that this man killed our father."

"That'll be enough out of you, Billy."

Billy, shocked by Johnny's lack of response, kept his mouth shut for the remainder of the night. They arrived to the signs notated on the map.

"It's a seven-day journey from here to the Forest Region, Billy. Once we get a little bit farther down this road, we'll rest for the night."

Billy nodded. As Johnny put away the map the brothers headed west, toward the Forest Region.

# Chapter 12

As Johnny and Billy walked, they spoke while they continued their way toward the Forest Region.

"Johnny, I've been meaning to ask, why did you loathe Ryan so much? He was our brother after all."

Hopefully he still is our brother. I hope he's all right.

"He got to spend more time with dad than I did. He was always getting the attention from dad and I just felt left out."

"Dad named you after him, that's got to mean something!"

"It does, of course. I'll never forget the day we got told Ryan ran away from home and then dad shifted all of his attention toward me—making sure I was the best."

"Do you think that's why dad left?" asked Billy.

"I don't know why he left, but I wish he were still here with us, Billy. I kept waiting for him to come back to see me off to enlist . . . but then I received that letter and that's when everything changed, as you know."

"That I do, Johnny."

"I just remember reading in dad's journal that he was always off on adventures with his friends."

"Wow, I didn't know that!"

"Yeah, there's a lot it seems we didn't know about our dad, Billy."

"It all seems like such a blur to me," said Billy, rubbing his temples.

"I'm sure it does, it was many waves ago. I remember that mom began going off on her own adventures and then one day she didn't return either."

"Ryan said she's in the Twilight Region, we should check there next!" said Billy.

"We most definitely will, after we take down this demon and make him answer for killing our father."

"I hope we're ready for this . . ."

"Do you remember the stories mom used to come back with and tell us?" asked Johnny.

"Not really, no."

"She used to recount to us her own adventures. Some by herself and some with dad and Uncle Dumont."

"Speaking of stories, tell me more about this Forest Region, Johnny."

"What did I say, Billy?"

"Johnny, I'm merely inquiring. Plus, this will pass the time on our journey there. So, do tell me more about this Forest Region."

"How do you mean?"

"Anything else about it!" said Billy, in a cheerful tone.

"I have no idea. The map isn't exactly as useful as I thought it'd be."

"I don't even know if dad made this map. He might have just gotten it from someone, a friend maybe, or maybe a merchant."

"What about this demon?" asked Billy.

"I'm not quite sure. He can't possibly be the sole inhabitant of a place as large as the Forest Region," replied Johnny.

"What happens after we find him?"

"After he is found, he is brought down," said Johnny, rubbing his eyes.

"Okay, then what? We just leave?"

"Get all the answers out of him possible as to why he killed dad."

"You don't think dad is still alive, do you?"

"He would have returned by now or reached out to us or something," said Johnny, letting out a big sigh.

"I suppose you're right. Crazy, isn't it?"

"What's crazy?" asked Johnny, throwing his head back, looking up at the sky.

"There's nothing really out here. Just a couple of trees every now and then."

"We'll keep going for a little more then rest for the night," said Johnny.

"Do you think we're getting close?" asked Billy.

"It hasn't even been a full day yet, Billy."

"Maybe so, Johnny, but still there's just emptiness. There are no buildings, cities, anything," said Billy.

"Well, all the other regions are on the opposite side of the Forest Region, besides the Twilight Region which I can't exactly tell where it begins. We happen to live on the East End where there is nothing but the Bulwark Bazaar and Candlelit Castle, and obviously Wakesfield."

"That map is really coming in handy, Johnny. I don't know what we'd be doing without it."

"Nor do I, Billy."

"When I was looking at it when you were sleeping one night, I was shocked to see the number of regions, there are five of them!"

"Well, there are five in this area of Direfell; there's the Forest Region, where we're headed now, then the Fire Region, the Ice Region, the Twilight Region, and one more that I cannot remember the name of. I believe it began with a 'W.'"

"The Water Region?" asked Billy.

"No, that wasn't it."

"Maybe if we keep whirling names around—"

"That's it. The Whirlwind Region."

"I would like to travel to all of the regions someday. With the family, you know?"

"Yeah, provided our brothers return from the war, dad and Derex come back to life and mom returns from her travels," Johnny answered sarcastically.

"Don't be like that, Johnny. It would be nice."

"I suppose."

"Do you know anything about these other regions? I mean, aside from the Forest Region that is," asked Billy.

"Can't say I do. If I were to speculate, based on the lay of the land, I would say the name of the region must have something to do with its layout. The Forest Region is obviously a giant forest, that extends on in what seems to be interminably. I can only fathom a guess that the Ice Region is covered in ice, the Fire Region is covered in fire, the Twilight Region is covered in twilight, and the Whirlwind Region is covered in—"

"In whirlwinds. Got it. I could have guessed so much myself."

"Hey, you asked, you got answered. Now we'll rest here for the night, behind these trees."

The two of them set down their gear and made rest behind the trees.

"I want to get in a lot more travelling and I'd rather not waste that time on sleeping. Once we get close enough to the Forest Region, we can rest up there on the outskirts. Until then, however, we'll just take breaks and sleep for a few hours here and there."

"We'd be better off with a full night's rest, Johnny."

"Strangely enough, I don't feel that tired."

"You know, now that you mention it, I don't either."

"I know we're used to walking a lot, but this feels different. Either way, get some sleep. We'll leave in a few hours."

As the two laid down to get some rest, some birds flew overhead and chirped, and as the hours passed, Johnny and Billy got the sleep they needed. Once they woke up, they continued their travel toward the Forest Region, and passed an occasional couple of trees, but nothing else besides the fields of grass.

The grass is unkempt and tickled their calves with each step. The ground welcomed their feet and smooshed in a little with each press of their boots. The only light guiding them were the luminous petals of silver twinkling above, which they ignored and pursued on.

Johnny pulled out the map once more just to take another look. As he did, he noticed something he hadn't before.

"The stars . . ."

"What, Johnny?"

Johnny stopped walked and shifted the map in his hands.

"The stars! They're revealing some kind of sign on the map. It's a tree branch and it's pointing to another entrance to the Forest Region."

"What? Let me take a look!"

Both Johnny and Billy looked at the map in amazement as well as the hidden message.

"There must be another entrance then."

"I would hope so, otherwise, why did that sign point this way?"

"Maybe to deter people who didn't have a map," said Johnny, still glaring down at it.

As they continued ahead, the brothers noticed more and more trees, signifying that they were drawing near to the entrance, and rightfully so as they took their sleeping breaks and pressed on day in and out. It had been five days of their seven-day journey.

When the brothers moved down, the field, plains of grass, and the trees started becoming larger and more brooding; the outskirts of the Forest Region and the Forest Region as a whole seemed to pull Johnny and Billy into its depths. There was no wind as they approached these larger trees as it was blocked out by the thick bark, branches, and the leaves. The sky above metamorphosed from a light blue to a vast, deep ocean blue. Johnny stopped walking, took off his bag and set it down beside him. He just stared up into the sky.

"Everything okay, Johnny?"

"Do we really not notice the sky that much?"

"What do you mean," asked Billy.

"I just mean, it's day, it's night, then it's day again. There's nothing to the sky it seems, and it appears to be constantly getting darker earlier than normal," said Johnny, motioning to the sky.

"We are in a different part of the land so maybe there is some time shift? Something of which we're not aware?"

"I don't know, Billy, it feels different than a simple time shift."

"Oh, trust me, time shifts are not as simple as one might think."

"What do you know about it, Billy?"

Billy finally caught up to where Johnny was stood and joined him when he gazed toward the sky.

"Oh just something I heard someone say once in Coheod Market," said Billy.

"Yeah. Right. Time worms and loopholes, got it."

Billy sighed at Johnny's ignorance.

"Are we spending the night here?" asked Billy.

"Very well. Maybe some sleep will do us good," said Johnny.

Both Billy and Johnny unpacked a sleeping throw from their bag, laid down on the ground and used their bag as a pillow and placed the sleeping throw over them. The grass came up slightly past the height of their bodies; they were almost covered by the grass like one would be if laid down in this field and wore all green blended in with the grass.

Billy stared with eyes wide open at the sky above—the stars began glistening as they sparkled off one another.

"I've never seen constellations like these before," said Billy.

"Nor have I, Billy. Goes to show just how far away we truly are from home."

One constellation formed what appears to be a bridge while another constellation formed a lightning bolt. Johnny scanned all of these constellations that slowly began to form in the sky above with a look on his face as if he just witnessed a dog that walked a human.

These are some odd constellations . . .

"Hey, Johnny?"

"Yeah, Billy?"

"Remember when Derex first said he was leaving for the war?"

"Yeah, of course, goodness, it's been so many waves. Let's see, I would have been eight, making you six and that would be putting Derex right at sixteen. Geez, we were just kids back then," said Johnny.

"Has it really been that long?"

"It would seem so. Now what about it?"

"Derex brought us all out to see the stars and told us that navigation was possible by them."

"Why're you telling me this, Billy?"

"Because if you look right there," Billy motioned his hand to a select set of stars, "You can see what appears to be two letters. I wonder if they're guiding us somewhere."

Johnny gazed in awe.

Those two overlapping 'M's are the same letters I saw when dad left. What do they mean?

"Get some rest, Billy, we're leaving early tomorrow."

"Oh good, something new. Us leaving early."

Johnny once again rolled his eyes at Billy's sarcasm before he slowly shut his eyes. The last thing Johnny focused his eyes on were the set of stars Billy pointed out—the ones appeared to have formed some sort of two letters. The two of them slept as the stars began to scurry away.

The letters in the sky above began to wane and dim away, as did the conscious stream of Johnny and Billy as they entered a deep slumber for the night. As the remainder of the stars washed away and the night turned into day, Johnny woke up.

His eyes shot open at the speed of a heavy rain that fell from the sky. He sat straight up and peered around, as if he was looking for someone, or something. He turned to Billy and gave him a little nudge.

"Billy, wake up, we're leaving."

Billy opened his eyes and rubbed them.

"That felt like a short snooze," commented Billy, as he yawned and stretched.

Billy rose to his feet and rolled up his equipment. The two of them then collected their gear. They continued to make their way toward the Forest Region.

It woke me right up, that shrill noise I heard. What was it?

Chapter 13

Deep within the depths of the Forest Region, there was a silhouette figure seated in a chair made entirely of stone. Not the same kind of stone of which Wakesfield was made. This stone was much different—it was lighter gray and much different to the touch. On its right was a shield, with a crest embroidered on it. The crest was made up of a man dressed in a ruby red robe going all the way down as to cover his feet. He had his eyes closed and had short brown hair, with a crown upon his head; the crown had many colored jewels embedded in it.

These colored jewels were a royal purple, sunflower yellow, fire red, stormy gray, burnt orange, ice blue, and onyx black. Next to this man with the crown was a black dragon with its tail wrapped around the feet of the man, or where the feet would be if the robe wasn't covering it. This black dragon's claw went across the man's chest, on the top right side.

The shield was in pristine condition and would glimmer if any light were to encroach through the canopy of the Forest Region. To the left of this stone chair was an incredibly sharp sword; three feet of cold steel with a fiery red blade. Its hilt was onyx black, with black straps wrapped around it.

The figure in the chair stared straight ahead and looked intently at whatever laid before them. This figure rang a bell—its sound was so shrill that it escaped even the silent miles of the dense Forest Region.

Back on the outside of the Forest Region, near the outskirts, Johnny ceased his walking.

"There it is again," proclaimed Johnny.

"There what is?"

"That tinging noise; it sounded like a bell or something."

"Now that you mention it, I did hear something."

"I wonder what it is."

"We must be getting closer as there are trees everywhere!" stated Billy, as he looked around.

"I think we're already here."

"You think so?" asked Billy.

"We must be."

Johnny and Billy took in their surroundings. What stood tall before them were dark, brooding trees that extend high up into the sky, so high in fact that the tops of the trees cannot be seen. The bark on these trees was so dark and almost black—much different than the lighter brown colored bark on the previous trees the brothers passed. The air around them was much denser than it was the night before and the air seemed cooler, despite there being no trace of wind at all. The trees did well to mask any sound came in or exited the Forest Region, unless it was the sharpest and shrillest of sounds. It was near impossible for any sound to enter the Forest Region and be heard as the trees would capture any sound and have it dismantled with their density.

"That's so odd!"

"What is?" asked Billy, with his eyebrows raised.

"The trees . . . I could've sworn I just saw clouds pass through them."

"The trees can't be that high . . . can they?"

They moved forward ever so slightly and cautiously another few steps. Johnny and Billy finally arrived at the outskirts of the Forest Region after seven long days of travel. The brothers stared in awe at the Forest Region, and it stared right back at them. Johnny had only heard stories of the Forest Region but didn't realize its intensity and height. There was an eerie silence between the two of them; they stood perfectly still and gazed at the Forest Region's infinite awe. Almost mesmerized and consumed by its entrance.

I knew it. We almost are in a different land—the sky hasn't been getting darker faster, it's just the trees that have been consuming the light from the sky due to their unimaginable height so much to the point that if a human were to attempt to climb the tree then fell, there'd be no hope for its survival. I don't even think birds would build their nests this high. Despite that, I still can't imagine them and they're right in front of me.

"Wow. I didn't realize we were that close. I guess we didn't notice it as it was so dark outside, ay, Johnny?"

Johnny continued his staring. He swallowed once ignoring the question of Billy—not because Johnny did not wish to answer, but because Johnny simply did not hear Billy as he was in his own world. Finally coming to, Johnny turned to Billy and stared at him for a moment. He assessed his body—his legs looked like wet noodles as did his arms. His neck was as thin as a pencil and his shoulders were about as broad as butter knife from top to bottom.

"Billy, I want you to wait here, on the outskirts, this is something I must do alone," said Johnny, with a hint of caution in his voice, "I don't want you to get hurt; you may only be in my way."

Billy turned to Johnny in shock and anger.

"He's my father too, you know. I want answers just as well as you! I want to fight the demon just as much as you!" said Billy.

"I understand, Billy. But this is something I must do alone. This is something I will do alone."

"Johnny, you have no idea what's in there!"

"It doesn't matter. My word is final and there is nothing you can do to change that."

"You need me in there and you know it."

"Like you just said, Billy, I have no idea what's in there. Ergo, I don't know if I'll need you, but in this particular case, it is better to not have you than have you."

"I don't believe what I'm hearing!"

"Then get a grasp on reality."

"Why're you doing this, Johnny?"

"Listen, I don't want anything else happening to another member of my family! You're too important to me and as of right now, here in this moment, you're all I have."

"Then let me come with you!"

"No, Billy."

"Why did you let me tag along then? Why did you even have me come with you?"

"I didn't know what to expect, and I knew you'd just follow me anyway. If you really want to help, then you can stay here. Or maybe, maybe you can return to the Bulwark Bazaar!"

"Back . . . to the bazaar. Are you serious? That's a seven-day journey, I'm not doing that."

"Someone has to let the people know that the Demon of the North will soon be slain! The demon's evil will be no more and will no longer pillage our city or the city of others!"

"Johnny, I don't even know what you're talking about. No one does. You're making no sense, so please stop now and just let me go with you. The demon has never even been in our city."

"Not that you know of, Billy."

"And what? You do?"

"I've come this far, and this is where the adventure begins . . . truly begins."

"Then let's begin it together."

"If we both go, we risk early detection. I don't want . . ."

"You don't want what? Me in the way? You think I'd really give away our position?" asked Billy.

"Enough. Just wait here. I'll even leave you the map. You can help plan out the next adventure to the Twilight Region to find mom when I return."

"*If* you return."

Johnny turned away from Billy and faced the Forest Region; its size was staggering as Johnny seemed like a twig on the ground compared to the size of the trees before him. Compared to Johnny, Billy seemed like a leaf on the ground.

Johnny entered into the tenebrous forest where when one looked up, even if the sun was shining, no light came through; it was a dark place where the trees' height dwarfed Johnny, with their seemingly endless canopy. The leaves in the trees high above the ground came together like if one clasped their hands in a tight formation around some object to be carried. The ceaseless ending trees formed deep down a barely visible dirt path. Johnny looked down this path and saw nothing ahead. No opening of light, no variance of a pathway . . . nothing.

It's impossibly dark in here, I hope my eyes will soon adjust otherwise, I'll be walking blindly.

This was the only path Johnny saw. He continued down this dark and brooding path and began his long journey to the North End. What Johnny did not know is the road ahead of him.

Chapter 14

The Forest Region—its large trees and lush undergrowth created a path which Johnny travelled. No light shined through the Forest Region—a giant canopy formed over one another, blocking any glimpse of light. The time of day meant nothing when one became engulfed by this shadowy forest. Beyond the barely visible dirt path before Johnny, there were trees that extended on for miles. Within this forest there are no birdsong or animal calls, not even the buzzing of insects. In the Forest Region, all Johnny could hear was himself think, much louder than normal. Its dense forestry and shrubbery surrounded the barely visible dirt path; the bushes were still—no leaves fell from the trees, no pieces of bark chipped off the large, brown trunks, despite their worn, withered, faded look. Everything in here appeared full of life.

The trees of the Forest Region are like castles, fortresses—the sleeping souls of them gave off this disturbing silence. So quiet that if the trees were actually alive, actually alive like Johnny, then he might have heard their pulsing hearts. They left no leaf-carpeted trail which to follow, but instead more of a mossy-veiled trail. The grass beneath Johnny's feet was crackly with each step due to lack of water. His awe continued at the size and majesty of the trees with their knotted arms rising ever upwards, as far as Johnny's head could tilt back. They were latened with moss of varying colors, which peeked out ever so slowly. The moss-covered bedding of the ground intertwined with the crackly grass gave off a musty fragrance. It reeked of age and its woody incense was from many waves of branches that snapped and plummeted to the forest's moss-covered floor.

My eyes . . . they appear to be adjusting to the darkness. I'm able to see, albeit barely.

Johnny slowly began walking forward through this verdant, ancient forest. He looked all over, scanned and surveyed every possible thing he passed. Sometimes it was difficult for him to tell where one tree ended, and one began due to his eyes which jumped from branch to branch. Every sprawled tree he passed under reminded him of some watchful guardian; a silent sentinel of the groves; a shifted sentry of the wood. His venture deeper and deeper into the tangled messy heart of this forest would be the ultimate test for Johnny being a kid from a city full of lights transitioning into a den of darkness.

The farther he entered, the more fantastical it became—the enormous brown roots spread and twisted around the ground, went under and over the moss-covered ground like a gopher that burrowed. The underbrush became thick and lush and formed an arch of sage green high above, almost like an entrance to another world. Arthritic boughs, gnarled with waves of stillness, greeted Johnny with each step. Bushes, hedges, and shrubbery flanked the trail, making it impenetrable on either side of the dirt trail, which forced Johnny to press on.

And again, my eyes are adjusting more and more. I feel like I've been in here for mere moments, but it must have been longer than this if my eyes are already adjusting.

Johnny made his way down this barely visible path before him. He moved slowly at first, traced each step and made sure he was fully aware of what he stepped on and around. Johnny was a careful one, but not so careful that he would delay his speed of movement, as he was spry when he must be, but slow with an abundance of mindfulness and finesse when called for. With each step, Johnny looked around to see if there was any substantial difference between the steps he took.

There is nothing around me. There is no difference in this place at all . . . The pathway's dirt is hard and old. This path has not been travelled on for at least two waves. I'm surprised the grass hasn't grown back over it and covered it up. Not that any water or sunshine arrives in this forsaken place of shadow and darkness.

Even though Johnny couldn't see it through the trees, he knew the sun would be setting about now.

I feel as if I've made no progress; that I've walked and walked down this dirt path and have not gotten anywhere. I know this isn't true for when I look back there is no light . . . no existence of anything behind me besides the trees. I should find a nice patch of grass to rest on.

Johnny continued to make his way down the dirt path and constantly looked around for any pattern of difference in this Forest Region. Much to his dismay, he again saw nothing but scattered trees, which disappeared off into the darkness into the hundreds, if he had to guess.

They form no clear path or direction.

He took a few more steps.

I've no idea what troubles await me in this place . . . this demon wouldn't be alone, would he? Not even a demon could control this whole region; it is far too large for any one being to control.

He proceeded farther down the dirt path then suddenly stopped. He peered through trees and saw something that caught his eye. Johnny arrived at a wide glade where the trees fell away and revealed an open grass area. The sap's sweet fragrance of the forest washed over him as he inched forward, seduced by its smell and comfort. Johnny closed his eyes and sniffed and as he did a smile took over his face.

Finally! I'll rest here until the sun rises . . . until I think the sun has risen, rather.

He looked around and made sure no one was around him, Johnny set down his gear and found his spot to rest. A light began to shine through the Forest Region's canopy. Johnny's eyes finally adjusted so much so that he was now prone to experiencing some gleam of light amongst the darkness. This gleam or ray of light only happened when one whose eyes have adjusted to the Forest Region's darkness, are inside one of the fields.

This new skill of sharpened, keen eyes allowed one to now see the Forest Region even brighter, as the farther in one travelled, the darker it seemed to become. Despite this new array of light Johnny experienced, he shut his eyes and fell off to sleep. He heard nothing. He attempted to lull to sleep at the sweet sound of emptiness—no birds chirping or animals snarling to disrupt his much-needed slumber. Just as he was on the cusp of falling asleep, high above the ground upon which Johnny laid, he was being watched. It was not long, however, before an arrow was shot at Johnny; he heard the bow string as it snapped into place as loud as thunder in the silence. This jolted him awake and without a second thought, he rolled out of the way and was able to dodge the arrow that thudded into the ground where he had lain a moment before. Despite this, the arrows kept coming at him.

An ambush? They're coming from all around me! But I don't see anyone . . . It can't be one person.

Johnny made a break for the trees in front of him. He quickly got behind a tree and peered out. As he did, an arrow flew by him. It barely missed him. He quickly hid his head behind the cover of the tree. Johnny dropped down rapidly, and sneakily, moved to another tree. He slowly peered his head out from the tree's cover. He did not even see a glimpse of a person as he looked high above to the trees. Johnny got fully behind the cover of the tree again and sat down.

I know there are people out there, but I just can't see them. They know I'm over here, but they don't know where exactly. It's time to face this. This is what I came here for.

Johnny rose, and while still behind the cover of the tree, Johnny called out:

"So, you can shoot at me from afar, which means you're all cowards and are hiding. Let's see if you can beat me up close," said Johnny.

Johnny peered his head out. When he did, a man dressed in camouflage came from the tree's canopy. All Johnny saw was his silhouette.

"This coming from a man hiding behind a tree. You talk a big game, so come on out and let's see what you're really made of."

"Call off your archers and I surely will," said Johnny.

"Archers? You think there are *multiple archers?* I am the only archer here."

"The only coward you mean," stated Johnny, coming out from behind the tree.

Johnny walked farther and approached the center of the grassy field. He saw a hooded, thin and muscular blonde-haired man with blue eyes and a blonde goatee. He was dressed in a forest green tunic. Resting on his back was a quiver of dark green. The tunic had a hood, which was currently up and worn. Along with this man's attire there were vambraces of camouflaged colors that displayed both forest green and dirt brown circular and ovular shapes.

This forest green tunic dropped down a bit past the man's waist and transitioned subtly into sage green pants, flexible for swift movement. Filtering down farther past the pants were dirt brown boots, which concealed this man's movement through the trees, and amongst the high blades of grass.

The man stepped forward and he took off his hood.

"I am no coward, you fool. I am Phoebus Ewing, legendary archer of these woods."

"If you're so legendary, how come I've never heard of you?"

"Ha, but a child's question you ask," replied Phoebus.

"But a question nonetheless. I'm here for one reason only."

"You'll have to beat the information out of me. And that is no easy task."

"Now who's talking a big game?" asked Johnny.

"Am I not standing here to fight you?"

"You're standing there," said Johnny.

"Quit talking then and let's get down to it."

Johnny and Phoebus stared each other down. Phoebus raised his right arm, extended it out and paused. He dropped his bow. They continued their stare down and Phoebus lowered his arm.

"I hope you're proficient in hand-to-hand combat, Phoebus."

"You have no idea."

Phoebus ran up to Johnny and threw a punch. Johnny quickly reacted and evaded this punch and dropped to his one knee. He then rose back up, formed a fist which he then threw at Phoebus.

Phoebus heard the whooshing sound and saw the speed that came from Johnny's punch, which allowed Phoebus to have moved to the left and throw his own punch at Johnny. However, Johnny saw Phoebus' aggression in his eyes as well as his formed fist out of his peripherals. He, too, saw the twist of Phoebus' shoulder and he lowered his elbow quickly to block the punch.

As quick as Johnny was to block the punch, Phoebus was even quicker to throw another one which Johnny could not block.

"Try blocking this!" shouted Phoebus.

Johnny dropped to his knees to avoid the punch, then dropped back to his hands and went to kick Phoebus.

"Nice try, but not gonna happen!" said Phoebus.

Phoebus caught Johnny's leg, twisted it and threw it to the left. Johnny, grunted, was quick to get up and threw another punch at Phoebus.

Johnny's punch was caught by Phoebus and he pulled him into his fist. Johnny grunted in pain, stumbled back, and clenched his stomach.

"Having trouble breathing?" asked Phoebus.

Johnny attempted to get up but could not due to the pain. He gasped for air. Having heard this, Phoebus ran at him and he flung some kicks, which Johnny tried to block. Due to Phoebus being unsuccessful with his kicks, he walked backward and allowed Johnny to rise.

"Had enough yet?" asked Phoebus.

"Not even close!"

Johnny proceeded to do a drop kick to Phoebus and hit him in the stomach, which knocked Phoebus down to the ground. However, he rolled on the ground and got back up, as did the blades of grass over which Phoebus rolled.

Both Johnny and Phoebus squared off in their respective stances. Johnny, in the way of the Black Dragon—a stance which its user had one arm extended out and the other tucked into their side. And Phoebus in the way of the Monkey—a stance where one had one arm bent into their body, and the other arm aimed up, rested their elbow on top of their fist, that made a right angle.

Johnny moved in and threw a punch, but Phoebus caught it and swung down his arm which was previously pointed upward. He then spun into Johnny's body used his elbow on the arm that was tucked in, which made contact with Johnny's diaphragm. Phoebus then stepped back, while he lowered his arm, and the force from this maneuver flipped Johnny over Phoebus' shoulder and down onto the ground, that made a loud slamming sound.

Johnny shouted out in pain when he landed hard on his back. Phoebus still held onto Johnny's fist after he flipped him and he went to stomp on him. Johnny reacted and kicked up his foot and hit Phoebus right in the face. He broke free from Phoebus' grip and rose to his feet.

Phoebus grunted, stumbled back, then assumed his stance. Johnny approached Phoebus and swung his foot quickly at Phoebus' face, which Phoebus evaded by ducking, and a loud whooshing sound from Johnny's kick was heard. However, Johnny was quick to bring his foot back the other way to hit Phoebus in the face with a loud bashing noise.

Phoebus spun backward and Johnny approached him and as he did, Phoebus threw an uppercut to Johnny's chin, he then spun around and extended his leg out, so his foot made contact with Johnny's stomach.

Johnny grunted, then stepped back but was quick and assumed his stance again.

"It would appear neither of us can get the best of one another," said Johnny.

"Then it's time to up the ante," said Phoebus.

Phoebus finally took out his twin daggers, twirled them in his hands which made a hissing sound from the speed at which he spun them. He then gripped them tightly. He slid one dagger over the other, each clean stroke gave off a clanging sound.

Phoebus' twin daggers had brown handles and were meticulously cleaned shiny blades. They came to a point and were in no way dull. They were small and lightweight enough to be thrown.

"What happened to a fair fight?" asked Johnny.

"There's no such thing. Do whatever you can to win. Especially when it's your life for which you're fighting."

Phoebus launched at Johnny with his dagger extended out and tried to cut him. Johnny saw Phoebus' movement and heard his feet as they pattered across the grassy ground. Johnny jumped back, rotated his body ever so slightly, then palmed Phoebus' right wrist, that made a small thud sound.

From this attack, Phoebus' dagger shifted, and Johnny landed on his feet, as did Phoebus. Phoebus spun around with the dagger in his left hand, extended, but Johnny bumped up his left elbow and made contact with Phoebus' wrist, and successfully stopped the attack.

Again, he spun the dagger in his hand but this time bumped Johnny's elbow with the grip and Johnny lowered his arm. Phoebus made a move toward Johnny and tried to cut him and was successful in doing so, but it was a shallow cut. Nevertheless, Johnny could still feel the warm rush of blood that dripped down his tunic.

Phoebus made a swipe toward Johnny's left arm with his one dagger in his right hand. Johnny evaded by leaning back and as he was about to kick Phoebus for a counter, Phoebus swiped at his arm again with his other dagger and shallowly cut him near the top of his arm.

Johnny ran back so Phoebus could not make any more hits, but Phoebus kept on with Johnny as he ran, as their boots stomped into the ground and ripped up blades of grass as they did. Phoebus began taking swipes at Johnny whenever he could

He's very swift.

Phoebus saw his opportunity to strike and stuck out his foot and tripped Johnny, but he rolled to get back up.

"Big mistake," said Phoebus.

As Johnny got back up after he rolled, Phoebus was quick and swiped his blade across Johnny's chest which made a loud tearing noise in his tunic. The blood from this cut seeped out onto Johnny's tunic. Johnny stumbled back and fell down loudly to one knee, thudding when he did.

Phoebus inspected the tip of his dagger and looked at Johnny's blood. He wiped it off on his boot, which made a crisp swiping noise as he did.

"Am I still just a coward?" asked Phoebus, "Where are your smart remarks now?"

Johnny, who was in pain, looked up at Phoebus. He could not rise and instead simply studied Phoebus and tried to analyze his next move. Johnny inquired and hoped to delay Phoebus with questions that would keep him at bay.

"A skilled fighter such as you in the Forest Region. For whom are you working?" asked Johnny.

"I said you'd have to beat the information out of me. Doesn't look like you're doing too good of a job with that, especially with all that blood you're losing."

"Maybe not, but you're not through with me yet!"

"Give it up before you die. I don't know what you came here to accomplish, but you're in the wrong area."

"If you think I'm finished then finish me. Come on!"

"If you don't take care of that cut, you will be finished. Why waste any more of my energy or time with you? In a few moments, you'll be dead anyway."

"You're not wrong. However, I would think that someone as legendary as yourself would want to finish me off. Unless you're not as legendary as your claim."

Phoebus, grasped his daggers more tightly and made a move toward Johnny. To Phoebus' surprise, Johnny rose and gave a roundhouse kick to Phoebus' left hand. Phoebus dropped one of his daggers, which hummed on its way down to the ground, before a loud stabbing noise was heard and it dove deep into the grass.

Phoebus then made a motion to stab Johnny. Johnny blocked the attack, grabbed his arm and twisted it down. Johnny then punched Phoebus right in the diaphragm, let go of his arm, and kicked him in the diaphragm which knocked him back.

Phoebus fell back and down to the ground. Johnny covered his bleeding chest with his hand and tried to suppress it. He then picked up Phoebus' dagger and approached him, gripping the dagger tightly as he went to stab Phoebus.

"This ends now," said Johnny.

Phoebus locked Johnny's legs in his own and swept him down to the ground with a loud boom as he landed on his back. They both rose, but as they did, Phoebus put away his dagger.

"If that's how you want it, then come at me!" proclaimed Phoebus.

If I can just make it to my bag behind the tree I can patch this cut up. If I go, Phoebus will just follow me. I need to end this. Now.

Johnny charged at Phoebus with the dagger, but Johnny's fist was caught by Phoebus' left hand. Just as before, Phoebus raised Johnny's arm, spun into his rib cage with his right elbow and threw Johnny over his shoulder. As Johnny was flipped over, so too was the dagger as it escaped Johnny's hands and landed on the ground. Phoebus drew his dagger and made a move for Johnny.

Johnny kicked back his right foot to Phoebus' face, spun around and picked up the dagger that fell when he was flipped by Phoebus. He swiped at the dagger in Phoebus' hand which made a clanging sound as the dagger vibrated and fell down and landed sharply in the grassy ground. Johnny put the dagger in his hand to Phoebus' throat.

Phoebus, in awe, ceased his fighting.

"You may think you're legendary, Phoebus, but you have never met someone like me. I'm a Hunderson, and I won't be so easily defeated."

"You're good, I'll give you that. I see there is no point in continuing this fight with you," said Phoebus.

"Said the man with his own dagger to his throat."

Phoebus leaned back, spun around to Johnny's back, grabbed hold of his arm that held the dagger and pushed him down to the ground on his knee and leaned into his ear.

"You have a long journey ahead of you before you reach Valmont and I wish you the best of luck."

"Valmont? Who's that?"

"You said you're only here for one reason," said Phoebus.

"How do you know I'm after Valmont? I'm seeking a demon known as the Demon of the North."

"Yup, that'll be Valmont. No one else comes into the Forest Region seeking anything else. Also, that's what I do. You wanted to know, so there it is."

"You do what exactly?" asked Johnny.

"I'm a sentry for Valmont. I'm supposed to keep people from ever reaching him."

"Then why even tell me his name?"

"Well, I don't particularly like Valmont, but I'm very good at what I do."

"Have you been successful in doing that? Protecting Valmont that is."

"Yes. Up until you, no one has ever made it past me. There's something different about you though. I sense you don't want to fight Valmont just to reign over the Forest Region."

"He killed my father, and I need to avenge his death."

"Revenge is not always the best path to choose."

"I don't need life lessons; I need to reach Valmont."

Although he has a point . . . No, no, I need to stay focused. My mission is bringing down Valmont!

"I imagine you know he's on the North End. What you don't know is what else lies ahead. I wish you the best of luck, uhm, I never got your full name."

Johnny walked up to Phoebus and extended his hand. Phoebus grasped it firmly and shook.

"Johnny. Johnny Hunderson."

"Johnny Hunderson, eh? I've heard that name before."

"That's why you stopped fighting, isn't it? You were just as curious for information."

"Maybe so."

"Either way, thank you," said Johnny.

"Best of luck, Johnny. Maybe we'll meet again under less complicated circumstances."

"Why not join me? Valmont is a monster, and I don't know how one could possibly work for him."

"Not everything is as it seems, Johnny. You know nothing about me."

"You weren't the first sentry, were you?" asked Johnny.

"No. Coming in the way you did, you missed some."

"How many more lie ahead?"

Phoebus gave a cold stare to Johnny.

"Until we meet again then," said Johnny.

Johnny turned around and walked away from this ground, continued on through the Forest Region where the path ahead seemed endless, and the trees whispered as an occasional breeze that crossed through their branches. He moved through the tall grassy areas and climbed over and through trees leaving a defeated Phoebus in the distance. As Johnny left, he risked a glance over his shoulder. The open grass area appeared perfect.

A worthy opponent, but what reason could a man of his stature possibly have working for a monster such as Valmont? At least I have a name now. Just have to put a face to it.

Johnny reached into his bag and pulled out some wrappings. He took off his shirt and wrapped tightly around his chest which allowed for nothing to get into it to get infected. Also, to have suppressed the bleeding in hopes it would have ceased all together. When Johnny put back on his shirt he realized how obvious the wrap was in contrast with his black shirt. He stomped the ground continuously with his foot and kicked up some mud. He spread it over the wrapping to darken its color a little, and hoped that whatever foes may lie ahead, if any, don't notice.

Johnny continued down this path and moved through trees, shrubs, and bushes alike. Each movement on this path became less and less visible, which indicated that none have travelled on this path before him. As he moved on through the Forest Region, Johnny's eyes became well adjusted to the darkness of the forest.

He arrived at a huge section of hedges. He looked to his left and his right there was no other way to go aside from through them. Johnny approached them slowly with his hand extended out, not knowing what was on the other side. His hand brushed against the hard, twiggy exterior of the hedges with their forest green color and razor-sharp leafy shell. Johnny's hand began to quiver as he pulled it back to his body.

Nothing is going to stop me. I'm going to do whatever it takes to make it to Valmont on the North End. I will not stop, no matter the cost. He will pay for what he's done.

With a light heart, Johnny plunged through into the over-arching vault of leaf, twig, and dirt that filled the massive hedges. When he arrived at the other side, it was not at all what he expected. The exquisiteness of the canopy's false light had not yet lanced to the lush, green sward and due to this nature, hoods of black shadow hung from the trees. The air here was much denser as coils of vaporous mist strangled the shaggy heads of the trees, writhed around them like one would when hugging someone.

It was both sensuous and illusory as sieves of fog caressed the lichen-encrusted bark, which added its phantasmal cover to the damp breath of the Forest Region and shifted from tree to tree like a monkey hopping around, if there were any monkeys in this desolate forest.

The mist deadened the sound even more as it haunted around and poured into the empty space and floated around. Then suddenly, a shot of supernal light peeked through the misty mesh and was soon followed by a whole loom of light, that gleamed down with its golden glow, and chased away the shadows as Johnny stepped farther away from the hedges.

The almond-brown trees stood awash with a tender glow as a soft amber light of luminescence touched their crusty exterior, which made the Forest Region much brighter now to Johnny than before, for the farther in he went, the more his eyes adjusted.

Johnny continued, moving past anything in his way and each step brought him closer to Valmont.

# Chapter 15

J ohnny continued his approach, stepped farther away from the hedges, and became entranced by the strange light. He stepped closer and descended deeper into the lush growth.

I must've been walking for hours now. At least my bleeding has stopped. I must find an area to rest up in, but there is just this emptiness ahead of me, a feeling like I'll never see the end of it. A forest full of nothing but trees as far as the eye can see.

Johnny lingered his walking for a moment.

What's this? Another open grassy area? I wonder if he has sentries stationed at all these open grassy areas. I best look up to the trees and make sure there aren't any archers up there.

Johnny took one more step up.

I guess there aren't any archers; they would've spotted me by now. Maybe my theory was wrong . . .

Johnny took another step and a staff with a blade attached to it, landed right in front of Johnny's feet.

"All right, quit your hiding; come on out and face me like a man."

"Who said I was hiding, kid?"

Johnny was swept off his feet and hit the ground. Johnny looked up and out of the tall grass emerged a man, he appeared much stronger than Phoebus with his thin, muscular build. Johnny quickly rose and faced this man.

He was dressed in a gray colored tunic. This tunic had a hood which was currently up, and shoulder pads, of a hard nature. The edging was hard as to ward off attacks from swords, arrows, and other forms of weaponry, but this particular style of tunic had a softer middle for the shoulder pads.

"Your tunic," said Johnny, "This style is traditionally done for someone who is an acrobatic and is more prone to rolling around to evade attacks."

"What's your point?"

"You don't strike me as the type," said Johnny.

"How about I just strike you instead?"

This man's tunic sat tightly and firmly at the waist, which allowed no fabric or article to have flapped around when he performed any sort of acrobatic maneuver. Right below the waist were similarly colored gray pants, which only stopped at the end of his legs to be greeted by his black boots.

"I am Richard Rendar. You triggered my trap, while I was waiting for you to enter; I merely concealed myself in the tall patches of grass," said Richard, lowering his tunic's gray hood.

"So, you're a wimp after all?"

"You might have been able to beat Phoebus, but I'm not such an easy adversary."

"We'll see," said Johnny, taking note of his short black hair and his eyes, his ice blue eyes staring right into his.

Richard picked up his staff with the blade attached to it and swirled it around and grasped onto it and squared off toward Johnny.

I'd better be careful. A swipe from that and I could be done for, not to mention if he has poison on the blade's edge.

Richard stabbed his staff blade outward toward Johnny, but Johnny caught it by the shaft and observed the edge of Richard's blade closely.

No poison, one less thing to worry about, I suppose.

Richard pulled back his staff blade, but Johnny was quick to release his hand as to not get sliced by it. Johnny then ran at Richard, but he took his staff blade and scraped Johnny right across the chest and extended the cut that Phoebus gave him with his dagger. This caught onto his tunic and ripped it even farther with a loud tearing sound.

As Richard swiped his staff blade, he spun and kicked Johnny in one fluid movement, and knocked him down on his back. Johnny was bleeding severely and was trying desperately to get up. He covered his injury with his hand, but he continued to feel the blood escaping from his wound and watched as it seeped out from around his hand. Johnny collapsed and passed out.

What is this? Is this real or a subconscious stream? Am I . . . dead? No, I can't be, I'm still in the Forest Region.

Johnny turned his head and just looked at Richard who looked back, right into Johnny's eyes with his soul-piercing ice blue eyes.

"Why didn't you finish me off?" asked Johnny, "I was unconscious, you could have easily killed me."

"That would have been too easy."

"Too easy?"

"Yes. You passed out after one swipe from my staff blade."

"So, you've spared me."

"Spared you? I'm just not finished with you yet," stated Richard in a menacing tone.

He'd rather let me come back to consciousness than kill me. He spotted my attempt at covering up my cut, but it doesn't matter now because I have an even longer one. I need to focus; I can't keep letting this happen. I'm a Hunderson and I'm better than this, my father trained me better than this! Even if the enemy has a weapon, hand to hand combat can still win the battle. If he cuts me again, I'm dead. No matter how unrealistic it is that I'm still alive as is, one more swipe and that's it.

Richard's ice blue eyes pierced into Johnny's as Richard continued speaking.

"No one skilled ever comes through here, you see. And if you've made it past Phoebus then you must be something special. No one has ever made it past him. That's not to say the first few sentries are easy, as I've seen people fail at the first one, but Phoebus is nothing to joke about. Nor am I."

"Fail at the first one? So, there are more sentries at the South End?"

"Correct."

"How many more?" asked Johnny.

"So many more that if you had managed to come through the South End, then you would have not made it to me, let alone Phoebus. Which means that you found another way in . . . how interesting."

"Why not have more sentries here then? That way no matter where people enter they won't be able to make it."

"The rule is one sentry per field, or so that's how it begins . . ."

"One sentry per field?" asked Johnny.

"Yes. There are many fields you skipped over by cutting through and entering from the East End. You missed one of my favorite sentries of all . . . Syra."

"Syra, huh?"

"Yes. Skilled with blades . . . Oh how I admire her work. You see, each of us sentries are skilled with at least one weapon, or in some form of combat."

"Why're you telling me all of this? I know I asked, but Phoebus didn't tell me anything," said Johnny.

"Unlike Phoebus, I won't allow to you make it to the next field. I have full intent of killing you, but it won't be as enjoyable for me if you don't have your strength back."

"I suppose a thank you is in order," said Johnny.

"Phoebus allowed you to pass for some reason, so he must have either seen something special in you or wanted to give the pleasure of finishing you off to me. And I intend to do so with those marks he gave you."

Just as I suspected. He easily noticed them.

"So, you basically just sit around day in and out in hopes that someone comes through your field so that you may kill them?"

"Essentially, yes."

"So, you took a job in which you would be allowed to kill people, is that it? Why not join the war?"

"A job is a job and this job pays well. Joining the war, I'd have to follow rules, wait for orders."

"Don't you do that here?"

"My orders here are simple: let no one pass. If I were to join the war, I'd need to be granted permission to kill. In here, in this job, it's welcomed. Now, enough chit chat, if you're able to speak you're able to fight. Let's have at it! No one has passed through these parts in a half and I'm eager to fight."

"Nothing is going to stop me," said Johnny, rising to his feet.

Johnny clenched his hand into a fist and tried to land a punch on Richard, but he saw it coming, and he jumped to the side. Eager to land a punch, Johnny turned around and again tried to punch Richard. Once more, Richard jumped to the side, only this time kicked Johnny in the rib cage.

If I try to punch him from afar, he'll jump to the side. If I get too close . . . he'll stab me with his staff blade. What do I do?!

"I'll never be able to have any fun if you're too afraid of my blade."

Did he just . . . No, he can't be a mind reader.

Richard stabbed his staff blade into the ground, took two steps forward and assumed a stance with both of his arms bent, one marginally behind the other, and his fingers somewhat curved in, almost as if he were making claws.

That's a stance from the way of the Wolf.

Johnny charged at Richard with his hand curled into a fist and punched Richard, but he caught his fist and lifted Johnny's arm and punched him in the rib cage numerous times. With each punch, Johnny grunted louder and harder.

Johnny pulled down on Richard's grasp of his fist and flipped him over onto the ground, making a loud thud as Richard's back slammed into the ground. Johnny then stepped on Richard's rib cage and pulled away his arm, and it made a loud cracking sound.

Richard was able to roll away and broke free of Johnny's grip. He got up slowly and assumed his stance again.

"You're going to pay for that," said Richard.

"Not likely."

Johnny charged Richard; however he spun around and delivered a back fist right to Johnny's face, that caused loud smacking sound to emanate from the contact, vibrating his face.

Richard then swung his arm and gave Johnny a right hook, followed by a left, once again it made his whole face feel as if he had been bombarded by strong ocean waves. Next, he followed up this hook combo with an elbow across Johnny's face, which caused him to temporarily see stars. Richard quickly concluded this elbow attack with another back fist.

Johnny stumbled back, shook his head quickly and tried to regain a sense of equilibrium. He came to his composure and threw a haymaker, yet Richard was quick to push away his forearm, then punched it, which caused Johnny to let out an involuntary grunt. Richard then kneed him in the stomach, then uppercut his chin, finished with a spin kick to his stomach, that knocked Johnny back toward Richard's staff blade.

Johnny breathed heavily, but each exhale was dampened by the trees. Johnny groaned from the pain. He tasted blood in his mouth as it began to swirl around.

"I told you, I'm stronger than Phoebus."

"Maybe a lot cockier than Phoebus, I'll give you that," said Johnny spitting out a bit of blood, "But that doesn't mean you'll stop me."

Richard's nostrils flared, before he let out a grunting roar. He then ran at Johnny and Johnny attempted to lift Richard's staff blade but couldn't because his rib cage hurting too much. He instead grabbed ahold of it and spun around and kicked Richard right in the face.

He stumbled back but continued to run at Johnny, which led him to repeat the same move.

"Novice," said Richard, rolling to avoid the attack.

Richard then kicked the staff blade, knocked Johnny off midspin, which forced Johnny to the ground. He rolled.

If I can keep him angry, maybe he'll make a mistake.

"You know, you keep saying you're better than Phoebus, yet I just don't see that from you yet."

"We're just getting started!" shouted Richard.

"Oh we are? That makes more sense then. Since you're a starter, maybe you should be moved to the field before, what was her name again? Syra?"

Richard removed his staff blade from the ground and assumed a stance with it. His breathing became heavier, and his eyebrows lowered more and more.

"You have no idea what you're getting into, kid!"

I think it's working.

"Clearly nothing much, since we're just getting started," said Johnny with a chuckle.

Richard bellowed before he charged at Johnny with his staff blade poised, ready to kill him. Johnny smirked and waited until Richard was about to make contact before he stepped to the side. Richard blew past Johnny and as he did, Johnny dropped to the ground, put out one foot and kicked the back of Richard's leg, and with the other foot, he tripped him down to the ground.

Once Richard landed on the ground, Johnny flung his arm out toward Richard's face with a back fist, that hit him directly in the mouth, and caused a buzzing and pulsing sensation in Richard's mouth.

Johnny did a kick up and landed on his feet then hovered over Richard.

"Looks like you lost. I guess you're not so *tough* after all."

"I haven't lost yet!" shouted Richard.

Richard rolled back and kicked Johnny right in the chin and knocked him down. Richard then rose and went to raise his arm but heard a cracking sound. Johnny heard this too and quickly rose and punched him right in the rib cage, breaking the rib he had fractured before. Richard collapsed to the ground.

Johnny walked over to him and extended his hand on down to Richard.

"You're done, I've broken a rib. There is no way you can possibly continue," said Johnny.

"You've only broken one rib. I can still fight you," Richard said, rising.

Johnny performed a spin kick to Richard's face and knocked him back down.

"Why not just kill me?"

"There is only one person's life I want. And that is Valmont's."

"You'll never make it," said Richard.

Johnny once again extended down his hand. Richard laid still almost as if he was frozen.

"I'll take my chances."

Richard grabbed Johnny's hand and is pulled up. When Richard was on his feet, he twisted Johnny's arm and flipped him down to the ground and pointed his staff blade at his throat.

"Many before you have tried to pass through here. Never have I had anyone break my rib cage. None of them even came close."

"That's because they had nothing driving them!" said Johnny.

"They wanted to bring down Valmont, just like you."

"Their reasons are not as great as mine."

"Revenge? You think you're the only person who has come seeking something like that? You're all out of reasons."

Richard moved to stab Johnny, but he quickly grabs onto the staff blade, by the blade, and pushed it off to the left. While he still held onto it, he pulled himself up and grabbed another part of the staff blade, by the shaft. He then forcefully pulled the staff blade out of Richard's grasp, spun it around and slashed at Richard's broken rib, which cut him deeply and forced him to one knee.

"Now we're finished! I don't have time to deal with a continual pest such as you," said Johnny.

"Anyone who can break my rib cage that fast is strong enough to move on ahead. You may proceed."

"I may proceed. What happened to killing me?"

Richard was silent.

Johnny took Richard's staff blade and threw it at Richard, and it landed sharply in the grassy ground right next to him.

"Have you ever considered leaving Valmont and joining forces with someone to bring him down?" asked Johnny.

Richard grasped tightly onto his staff blade and slowly rose and got back up to his feet. As he did this, he gave Johnny a cold stare, just like Phoebus did. He then rushed at Johnny with his staff blade in his hands, aimed to kill Johnny. Johnny easily grabbed hold onto Richard's staff blade, strongly taking it from his hands, once more.

He then used it to trip Richard down to the ground and smacked him across the face with the blunt opposite end of the staff blade.

Richard, now truly looking defeated, who steadily bled from his side and with no more tricks up his sleeve, turned his head toward Johnny. He relayed to him one line as his ice blue eyes gazed into Johnny's eyes.

"My brothers are up ahead, good luck with them."

Johnny took the blunt end of the staff blade and knocked Richard over the head with it, which knocked him out cold. Johnny dropped the staff blade down next to Richard and walked over toward his bag and grabbed it.

He then made his way back over to Richard and knelt next to him. He pulled out some wrappings and tended to Richard's wound. Johnny breathed heavily and grunted as he fixed Richard up, as he, too, tried to recover from his own wounds.

I'm no murderer, but if the only option to pass a sentry is to kill them, then I must find another way. I can simply maim or incapacitate them. The only person whose life I'm taking is Valmont's . . . A life for a life.

Johnny rose, clutching his rib cage in pain. He double wrapped his own wound. He made his way away from the field, leaving an unconscious Richard defeated.

He got me really good. He almost broke one of my ribs! And what did he mean by brothers? How many are there?

Chapter 16

Though the path was dark, cast into the shadows by the tall moss-covered trees on either side of Johnny, the sun must be brilliant beyond it. The forest was now even quieter than it was before, due to the thickness of the trees.

The trees in this part of the Forest Region began to dance as their leaves fell silently to the ground. One leaf landed on Johnny's shoulder and he looked up—he became almost transfixed by the myriad of leaves that flurried and that shook high above in the boughs, and almost made a roof above his very head. The longer Johnny stared at the leaves, the more the leaves seemed like eyes that stared back down at him. He felt as if he had almost fallen with them and got weak in the knees and trembled. Johnny pulled out some water from his bag and sipped it slowly.

Each tree glows a bright green just at the edges of the trunks; a glowing ring of sorts that brings a soothing happiness I've been missing these past few days. I do wonder how Billy is doing . . . Surely if I brought him along he would have been able to dodge all of these attacks which clearly, I cannot.

Johnny passed by montane trunks that appeared impenetrable. He eventually traipsed to one and brushed his hand against its rough exterior. As he did, sap trickled its way down from the tree and onto his hand. He rubbed it off and it hit the mud. As it did, the mud became an obsidian color. He looked inquisitively at the change to the mud.

Johnny took more sap and spread it on the mud beneath his boots. In seconds, the mud again turned to an obsidian color. He quickly scooped up this mud and rubbed it all over his wrappings, so they blended better with his black tunic. He continued to look around and stumbled upon pine needles. He picked them up, as well as some of the fallen leaves, and put them in his bag. Johnny continued through the Forest Region, and climbed over trees and any obstacle that got in his way. While still clutched onto his rib cage, he attempted to climb up a tree to see if he can see ahead at all.

Much to his dismay he could not, due to the pain. Plus, all he could see ahead were hordes of trees. Remembering what Richard told him, he clutched his rib cage, and looked for a place to rest. Johnny glanced to his left and saw nothing, but when he looked to his right, he saw a small alcove with a mossy exterior.

Johnny walked over to the rock and laid down under it and shut his eyes to get some rest. He tried not to move and knew that if he did, he would feel pain in his rib cage. So, Johnny just laid under the mossy rock and fell asleep.

As he drifted off into a deep slumber, he encountered a nightmare, which had never happened to Johnny before, as he usually hadn't gotten enough sleep to have nightmares, or even dreams for that matter.

In this nightmare, Johnny assumed a body of someone who walked toward an abundance of trees—it was the Forest Region this body walked toward. Johnny seemed to be in control of this body's movements at first, but ultimately, he came to the realization that he was not, as this being moved entirely on its own.

This being started to move its hands together, and as they touched, the being formed different signs, like a spellcaster of some sort. One of immense power, for the ability to make the land rumble was not some easy feat.

Colors started spurring out this figure's hands and flowed through their arms and soon all around them. Trees began to collapse, and pounded down one directly after the other, almost as if they were tied together and someone pulled them. Johnny now fully knew he was not the figure, stood in amazement, awe and watched this figure performed this action. Johnny tried to move closer, but couldn't due to some form of paralysis cast unto him either by his own shock, or by the spellcaster themselves.

Johnny opened his mouth and tried to beckon a call to the spellcaster, but to no avail. Nothing came out of his mouth aside from his breath which seemed to trickle before him, teasing him with its ability to freely move before it froze, fell to the ground, and shattered into tiny pieces.

These tiny pieces slowly rose and moved toward the spellcaster and began to form something in their right hand. Johnny, intrigued more and more by this tried to turn his head to have seen even more of where these particles were going. As he did, one of the collapsing trees came right for him and fell on him, it made everything black and dark.

Johnny shot up, barely missed his head hitting the arched stone covered in moss. His chest pounded, and his heart is raced. He looked around to see if any of the trees that surrounded him fell. He couldn't believe that this was just some nightmare he endured; he knew for sure this was a real occurrence. He just couldn't fathom what happened to all of the trees that fell . . . He was in the forest, around to hear them, but they made no sound.

That . . . that was a dream after all. Or a nightmare, rather! Having that tree collapse on me like that, I was a goner for sure.

Johnny slowly lowered his body back down under the arched stone covered in moss and closed his eyes once more. This time he slept deeply and soundly, with no worry or nightmares of collapsing trees.

The next day Johnny awoke and sat up under the rock. He reached into his bag and pulled out some water and food. He also pulled out the collected pine needles and leaves. He rolled them up and crumbled them down onto his food. He then took some sap and spread it over his food as well. Johnny quickly consumed his food and washed it down with water. He was not ready to go on but prepared himself nevertheless.

Johnny, convinced he was ready, rose and continued to travel through the Forest Region. He took one more look around to see if there were any changes to the lay of the land.

There's nothing . . . No difference at all. No leaf out of place from when I had fallen asleep two days ago, almost as if time had slept with me.

Johnny, moved slowly and cautiously through the depths of the Forest Region and looked around for markers of any kind.

It would appear as if the pain from my injuries has subsided. Could there be something in the sap? Some healing agent?

The dirt path beneath his feet slowly vanished. He was stepping on full areas of grass.

I guess I'm the only one who's made it this far. Right up until now there was a dirt path which I could follow, barely visible as it was, it was still something. Even so, Phoebus said no one has made it past him so maybe it's from the other sentries.

Johnny continued on what he felt was straight ahead, the full areas of grass flourished before him, almost welcomed him with each step as the blades of grass crawled higher and higher up his leg. He quickened his gait just a few more steps, and as he did he stumbled upon yet another open grass area. Johnny was extremely cautious this time.

He peered his head around the side of the tree ahead to see if any traps were lain or if there was anyone up in the trees high above. When he did this, he saw someone sitting in the grass. They're barely visible as the grass here was tall. Johnny snuck in past the trees and ducked down in the grass and slowly approached the person.

This grass gets taller with each open grass area. Pretty soon it'll be well above my head. I barely saw this person—they look like the top of an onion growing out of the ground.

Johnny tried to move slowly and seemed to snap each twig he stepped across. These snapping twigs were as loud as a crow's caw in a cathedral. He kept his eyes on the figure, as he tripped over some tree roots that grew of the ground. He caught his balance before falling.

Clearly being cautious is not my forte today.

Johnny took another step.

"You can stop right there," said a voice from up ahead.

No way anyone could see me yet.

"If you continue any farther you will force me to get up and attack. I don't like fighting people unless they're at their full potential, and it would seem that you're not . . . Johnny."

"You have me at a disadvantage. You know my name, but I do not know yours . . . friend."

"My name is Simon Nomis. As you can tell, I am much older than those you've recently encountered."

"Actually, I can't tell anything yet."

Simon rose slowly while clutched onto a black cane. He was dressed in a black colored tunic, like Johnny. This style of tunic extended down to the waist, where it was tucked in tightly. This, much like Richard's style of tunic, was for those who are acrobats. Beneath the black tunic were black pants, followed by black boots. Johnny assessed this man's tunic and a slight grin cracked on his face.

Well, he has good taste.

"I am Valmont's next sentry."

"You don't look that much older," commented Johnny.

"I didn't mean I was an old man. I meant I'm older than the rest. That means I have more experience and wisdom on my side," said Simon, coughing profusely and clutching his leg.

As he covered his mouth, he placed a pill between his teeth. Johnny stood still and stared, took note of Simon's cough and leg he clutched as well as the pill he consumed.

"The only thing you have on your side is a near broken rib," said Simon.

Johnny, not wanting to encourage Simon's correct guess, said nothing.

"Your silence doesn't make it any better. No answer is as good as any, Johnny. Plus, that sap of yours is beginning to fade. Its color only lasts for a short amount of time. In case you didn't quite pick up on how things work here, yet, that sap has healing powers."

"So it does have healing powers?" asked Johnny.

"Yes. It has rapidly improved your recovery speed. Come now, you didn't really think that someone as beat up as yourself would recover so quickly. This isn't some fantasy story you're living, Johnny."

"Sure."

"I don't know what is going on through your mind, and I really don't know what's going on through Richard and Phoebus' minds, but you're not leaving this area unless you kill me."

"I'm no killer. I'll find a way to get past you without killing you."

"So you say, but it doesn't matter . . . The time is coming anyway."

"What time?" asked Johnny.

"The time for our fight to commence."

Johnny made no sudden movements. He was as still as he could possibly be. Even stiller than he was in his nightmare. Not a single twitch or flutter arose from Johnny.

I didn't come here for anyone other than Valmont. I have to do this.

Johnny flicked his fingers and Simon instantly charged at Johnny, took swipes at Johnny with his cane, but Johnny caught the cane with ease, and pushed down. He then swung a leg over it then spun around and knocked the cane out of Simon's hands.

Johnny squared up and threw a straight punch at Simon and made direct contact with his face. Simon, seemingly unphased by this attack, forced Johnny to throw another one. This time, Simon caught his shift, then dropped down and monkey-flipped him over his body.

Simon rose and grabbed his cane, then beat Johnny mercilessly. Johnny, finally able to have rolled out of the way, rose back to his feet. Simon grabbed the cane with a second hand and swat Johnny, hit him once, and as Simon aimed to do this again, Johnny grabbed the cane with both hands and overpowered him.

With possession of the cane, he swatted Simon across the face to the left, then back again across to the right. He then spun and extended the cane at the end of his arm and smacked him once more across the face. He then juked Simon's hand and swept him off his feet.

Johnny straddled over Simon and began choking him with his cane.

"You can't force me to kill you, but I can stop you," said Johnny.

After he choked Simon for a few moments, Johnny released the cane from his throat and checked for a pulse. He felt a faint one. He rose and turned away.

Simon hooked Johnny's foot with his cane and pulled it back, and his face slammed down to the ground and made a loud thud.

"Not quite long enough, boy!"

Simon rose and jabbed his cane on Johnny's back, and followed this move up as he scooped up Johnny's legs and pressed them down hard with his cane. Simon pulled out some rope and tied Johnny's legs to the cane and subdued him. He then purposefully faced the loop of the cane out.

"If you're not prepared to kill me, then you will die," said Simon.

"I thought you were unconscious," said Johnny, squirming.

"Come now, Johnny, I thought you were smarter than that."

"It's that pill you took right before we fought, isn't it?"

"Just like I said . . . you're smarter than that. Exactly. The pill."

"And that's why you waited for a moment before we fought, for it to begin its effects."

"Correct. I may as well tell you since you're not going to leave this place alive," said Simon.

Johnny stopped squirming and looked at Simon as he tried to take in what he had said.

"You mean to tell me there are pills that cause a temporary state of paralysis?" Johnny asked.

"These pills are made from the sap extracts, but these pills work much quicker than the sap itself," Simon explained.

"That must be why I healed so quickly, just like you said."

"Why of course! In what world can someone have their ribs near broken and be ready to move merely in two days? Hmm? In what world can someone lose so much blood and still be able to fight, let alone stand?" questioned Simon.

"Then I really did die back there with Richard. I'm . . . this . . . Where am I?" asked Johnny, frantically.

"Why you're in the Forest Region, Johnny," replied Simon.

"This isn't real. What did you do to me?"

"Oh of course it's real, Johnny. It's all real. Everything you feel and everything you don't. It's all real."

Johnny wiggled around more on the ground and realized that the curved part of the cane faced out. He slowly squirmed toward Simon's feet, and in one quick swoop, he hooked onto Simon's ankle, then gave a hard yank which knocked Simon down to the ground. Johnny rolled around and reached onto Simon's person to see if he had any sort of sharp object.

"Roam all you want to, Johnny. But you'll never escape this field."

Johnny felt a blade and yanked it out of Simon's pouch. He then cut himself loose and rose up to his feet. He stood tall over Simon with the blade in his right hand.

"I am not long for this world, Johnny. And I no longer have any desire to be a part of it. You will kill me either by your own design or by my force."

"I will not kill you. I am leaving now so just let me pass."

"Afraid to kill?"

"I came here for one man and one man only. I came here to bring down Valmont."

"And what do you think bringing down will entail?"

Simon rolled back and quickly rose and threw a punch. Johnny stepped back, swiped at Simon's arm, and sliced it. He then grabbed onto Simon and threw him back down to the ground.

"A life for a life is just and fair to Valmont's end. I will not kill those just because they stand in my way."

"What kind of sad revenge story is that?" asked Simon.

"Revenge isn't always the best path to walk," said Johnny, "I'm leading my own, new path of justice. I will kill when I have to, not when I want to."

"The best path to walk? It would appear that Phoebus' philosophies have gotten to you," commented Simon.

"He has an excellent point. And even more so, I don't understand why any of you are working for Valmont."

"Why and for whom I work is none of your concern. It is a job."

"Now you sound like Richard . . . I'm through with this fight. You may do what you wish, but I'm walking away."

"Oh, you're walking away, sure, but not without killing me first. And if you don't kill me, I will kill you!"

Johnny clenched the dagger in his right hand more tightly.

"This fight is over, Simon!"

"To reach Valmont you *will* have to kill people. And to beat Valmont, you will have to kill him. And to continue farther . . ."

Simon locked his legs in with Johnny's then tripped Johnny.

Johnny fell straight down on top of Simon, which forced the blade into his chest.

". . . you'll have to kill me."

Johnny quickly rose, then fell back. He stared directly at the blade now plunged into Simon's chest. Simon's breathing became heavy, before it faded away to a slow, soft breath, which became softer and softer.

"I wanted to know why my father was killed. I didn't want to become the very thing I despise. Even if I tried to patch him up, he would not survive. That cut was too deep."

Johnny grabbed Simon's cane. Before he left, he stared at Simon one last time. He walked up to him and rips off a large piece of his tunic. He took this piece of Simon's tunic and tied it around his own, where it was ripped. He then did the same thing for his arms.

With the luck I've been having, I best take a few pieces of scrap, just in case.

He turned and made his way toward the North End of the Forest Region and left a dying Simon on the grassy ground behind him. As he did, something unusual happened. When Simon drew his last breath, a beaming, blinding, golden light shot out and shone bright from his chest. Johnny turned back around to see this light, but it was too bright for his eyes to take in.

With his curiosity piqued, Johnny approached the lively light.

With his arm held in front of his eyes, he tried to block some of it.

What is this?

As Johnny took a step closer to Simon's body, he reached out his hand and tried to touch the light. He was suddenly flung back and landed hard on his back with a loud thump. He tried squinting his eyes and looked again, but to no avail. Instead, he made for farther travel into the depths of the Forest Region.

As he ventured farther and deeper into the Forest Region, a few mere moments later, the beaming light that emitted from Simon's chest slowly, very, very slowly, began to fade and wane away. The once translucent light now became more transparent, as it got even softer and softer, it faded away almost as if being sucked up and swallowed by the Forest Region's shrouding darkness and its canopy. By this point, Johnny had limped much farther on. He was now getting used to having a cane by his side but was not very happy with the fact that he was using one.

This cane will help mend me back to health as not so much pressure will be on my ribs. I will look for a place to rest.

Johnny maneuvered through the Forest Region and discovered a patchy grass area. He collapsed once he got to it. He saw some sap and consumed it. He pulled out his water, took a sip, and put it back in his bag then passed out. Time within the Forest Region seemed to linger on and never passed by, as Johnny finally woke and looked around, he felt as though it had only been moments.

In actuality, and unbeknownst to Johnny, he had fallen asleep for two whole days. His pain was far too great to wake up from any deep slumber and this deep sleep was exactly what he needed to feel better rested.

Johnny opened his eyes wider and looked around again, only this time more warily. He slowly rose up from the patchy grass area upon which he slept and pressed against his rib cage.

This still hurts quite a bit, but the pain is slowly subsiding. I really wish to put a patch on the area, but any sign of weakness is exactly what these sentries are trained to go for. Doing this would be like having a giant target on my back. It's already sketchy enough having these extra wrappings tied around my body.

He reassembled his gear and continued his travel through the Forest Region. As he did, he heard a faint noise in the distance. Almost like a deer trenched through shrubbery and snapped twigs with each trapse.

What was that? There are no animals here . . . it must be someone.

Johnny went to investigate, but saw a branch snapping off from one of the trees as it quickly dropped down to the ground, scratching against other branches and limbs as it did, and snapped twigs.

If what Simon said is true, and I am in some different world, then I don't know if I should push myself to the fullest of my limits. I would like to believe what Simon said to me was some scare tactic . . . But if this isn't, and I really am in a different world, then why is my pain not yet fully healed. Or maybe, just maybe, he was a spellcaster like the one in my nightmare. And I was potentially under some trance in which I felt as if I were part of another world. Either way, I don't understand and no longer have any desire to think this matter. However, the mysterious shining light that seemed to have come out of nowhere is definitely something to look into.

Johnny pressed on through the lush undergrowth of the forest's ground. The grass was now well above his knees and crept slowly higher to his hips. This part of the Forest Region was dominated by bushes, shrubs, and hedges alike. All of varying heights and shapes— one such area was even a darker shade of green than the others, a jasmine kind of green. Johnny scrambled onward to the bushes in front of him. They were full of fresh berries, blue and orange in color.

An unusual color. I've never seen berries like these before.

Johnny grabbed one and ate it and tasted its juicy sweetness. It was like drinking an ice-cold glass of freshly squeezed lemonade, sprinkled with just the right amount of sugar. He took out the blade he liberated from Simon and used it to cut down a bushel of berries.

As he did, he saw another open grass area through the bushes, and he slowly pushed through them and approached the open grass area. He knelt down when he reached it. When he poked his head out, he saw not one, but three silhouettes that stood in the shadows.

Johnny took the cane and placed it lightly down on the ground next to him. He inhaled through his nose and exhaled through his mouth, slowly. He rose and approached the silhouettes.

 *Chapter 17*

J ohnny crept confidently toward the figures. His shoulders were thrown back and his chest was puffed out. While he tried to act fierce, he made a remark toward the silhouettes.

"You must be the brothers about Richard was speaking. Bring it. Come and attack me with everything you've got!" said Johnny.

Johnny took a couple of more steps forward and saw the three brothers just stood there, waiting.

"Someone is in a hurry to die."

Which one said that?

"Now that would be rude. Let us introduce ourselves. I am Captain Anthony Rendar."

Johnny quickly examined all three of these brothers and made sure none of them went to make a move toward him. He then looked back at Anthony.

This man wore a navy blue tunic, which was exactly like the one Richard had on, despite its color. The tunic met at the waist and was tucked in neatly and tightly. The pants Anthony wore were also navy blue, and the boots on his feet were black.

The shoulder pads had a hard exterior but were padded and soft which allowed for him to have rolled on the ground and not hurt his shoulders on impact. There was a patch on his upper left shoulder, as well. On his right forearm, there was a wrapping with a blade attached to its exterior. This blade would gleam in the sun due to how clean and well kempt it is, if there were any sun that shined through this canopy above that is.

On his hip rested his belt which had a sheath attached to it. Inside that sheath was his sword—this sword's blade was around three feet and was as sharp as his arm attachment.

"I am the oldest offspring of the Rendar family, and I am able to conquer anything, or anyone."

An A.C.P.F. patch? He's in the A.C.P.F.?

"I'm in the Army Commando of the Protective Force," said Anthony.

I wonder when he'll stop babbling and let the next one talk. However, as long as they're talking, maybe my rib cage will heal completely from that sap.

"My name is Dash Rendar, second oldest to the Rendar family."

What is he wearing? Wait, I've seen that attire and stance before, he must have studied in the way of the Tiger. And great, he's thin and muscular. I thought Richard was bad enough, now there are three of them. Those gray eyes of his, he seems like he's . . . elsewhere.

Dash was dressed in a maroon tunic. Unlike his brothers Anthony and Richard, Dash did not have the shoulder pads attached to his tunic; he removed them some time ago as he thought of them as nothing more than getting in the way.

Laced into his waist was the tunic, and directly beneath that were his maroon pants, which came down to his black boots. Attached to a belt on either side of his waist were batons, at approximately an arm's length. These batons were maroon and matched Dash's tunic and they sat in their respective holsters, attached to his belt.

"You may have beaten Richard, but that is nothing hard to do."

"Such confidence in your brother . . ." said Johnny.

"Well, you're here, aren't you?" replied Dash.

"Why was he placed all the way back there and you up here?"

"It goes by skill. The more skilled you are, the closer you are to Valmont," said Dash.

"Unless he's pretty much right after you guys, then that means you aren't as skilled as you think."

"You were able to make it past Simon . . . I suppose what he said about his illness was true," said Anthony.

"He was dying, wasn't he? That's why he forced me to kill him!"

"Right, because as we've been told, you haven't killed anyone yet. Well, I guess that's not true anymore, is it? You didn't want to kill anyone . . . This should be an interesting fight," said Dash.

"We'll see how interesting since I made it past Richard," said Johnny.

Dash reached for a baton. Anthony stopped him.

"Got someone upset I see," commented Johnny.

"You haven't seen yet," replied Dash.

"So, the more skilled you are the farther back you're placed. Seems simple enough."

"So simple to the fact that you skipped past a ton of sentries and the very fact that you beat Phoebus and our brother must mean you must be somewhat skilled," said Anthony.

Johnny smirked.

"Then again, we're all extremely skilled and if you had entered through the South End of the Forest Region, I have no confidence that you would have made it past Syra," remarked Anthony.

"Everyone speaks very highly of her. Some blade expert," replied Johnny.

"*A* blade expert. If you want *the* blade expert, then allow me to introduce myself."

Right then, last one.

Johnny looked over to the final brother. He assessed him as he began speaking.

"I am Jake Rendar, second to youngest."

Jake Rendar, dressed in a sage green tunic, with his shoulder attachments removed. Like the rest of the Rendar family, their tunics were custom made with the special shoulder pads and the ability to remove them as they saw fit. Jake had his off as he, like Dash, enjoyed the freedom that allowed his arms to be moved straight up without the slightest resistance, not that the shoulder pads gave off any resistance to those moving their arms, because they followed the flow of the arm.

I'm not even surprised that he has black hair, honestly. You'd know they were a family even if . . . what's he murmuring about?

"I have acquired a special set of skills that you may find hard to beat."

Johnny barked, "Let's get this thing started, I have someone to destroy."

"As you desire," Jake said chuckling.

Jake charged at Johnny, so he quickly dropped his bag off his back. Jake rushed in and laid some vicious combos of attacks, with triple kicking to multiple punches at once. Jake continued to punch him swiftly in the rib cage, but Johnny could not block his attacks quick enough. Johnny stepped back and coughed, loudly. Jake then swept him, and he fell to the ground.

Spinning kicks, sweep tactics, what's this guy in? Wait. Special set of skills. S.S.S. It can't be; this kid is in the Special Snake Service? No wonder why Valmont hired all these people; they're so strong. And the A.C.P.F. guy. I wonder if he served with any of my brothers.

Jake got quite a few hits in on Johnny until he rolled back and got up off the ground. Jake swept him, and he again fell to the ground. Jake again, laid vicious combo attacks on Johnny, who avoided the last few punches, kicked Jake off him and rose.

What am I going to do? He's moving so fast I don't even have time to think of an attack.

Jake spun and kicked Johnny in the face and he stumbled back.

Or maybe that's just it, I don't plan, I just rely on random attacks. Now!

Johnny aimed a punch at Jake's face, yet Jake was quick to evade and counter. He grabbed Johnny's fist and flipped him over, and he rose with a punch aimed for Jake. He stepped to the side and kicked Johnny in the stomach, then he grabbed him and shoved him down.

He dodges as well as Billy. Better even because he counters, too!

"Let's ramp this up a bit, shall we," said Jake, pulling out his blades.

Johnny rose once more, this time he went in for a kick, yet he was surprised by Jake's next move. He leaned into the kick and ducked down to dodge it, rather than having leaned back. Johnny brought his leg back toward Jake.

Jake still ducked down, turned to his left and leaned back toward the kick. Johnny's kick went over Jake as he leaned back. Jake did a backflip and pushed back Johnny's leg with his two feet. He then turned into Johnny and gave him and uppercut with the blunt ends of his blades, then a spin kick to the face that knocked him down.

Johnny didn't rise this time. He rolled away from Jake and laid on his back and looked back toward Jake. He stood still. He then slowly slid one blade down across the other, much like Phoebus did with his twin daggers. Clanging them with each stroke, hissing as one blade slid down across the other.

Johnny got up slowly and moved back toward his bag and pulled out his water and took a sip. As he put the canteen back in his bag he realized that Anthony was no longer standing where he once was. Johnny looked up and saw Anthony standing over him. Johnny tried to get out of the way, but Anthony bear hugged him and slammed him down, which caused a loud thud. He then lifted up Johnny's bag and chucked it across the field, far out of Johnny's reach. Johnny got up quickly and squared off against Anthony. As he did, Anthony pulled out his sword.

"Has no one here ever heard of a fair fight?" asked Johnny.

"Why fight fairly when our job is to maim our prey?"

"Maim? Richard said to kill."

"Richard has a few wires loose, but our job is to simply maim you so much to the point that you either turn back and leave or keep on going and risk dying due to injury. So Richard was technically correct."

"Well I'm not turning back!" shouted Johnny.

"Then I suppose this is where it all ends for you," said Anthony.

He walked toward Johnny with his sword, swatted aimlessly through the air, which created loud whooshing sounds. He then spun the sword once in his hand as he got closer, then slashed down toward Johnny.

"Your speed is hindered by that thing," said Johnny, stepping out of the way of Anthony's attack.

"But my reach is extended," replied Anthony, slamming the hilt back at Johnny's chest, making contact.

Anthony then turned the sword and grazed Johnny's leg, and he felt a sharp sting. He looked down at his leg, then heard the pattering of footsteps that ran at him. He looked over his shoulder and saw Jake as he moved in toward him.

Johnny extended out his leg and went to kick Anthony, but he caught it and kicked out his other foot and knocked him down. He rolled out of the way and rose and threw a swift punch at Jake which knocked him back, but not off his feet.

Both Anthony and Jake charged in at Johnny, but he stepped back which allowed their respective weapons to have clashed and clanged against one another. Johnny then quickly used his force and slammed their hands down to the ground, and that allowed gravity to do its work.

"Foolish mistake," said Jake.

Jake then slipped out one dagger, flung it in the air, then used his shoulder to bump it toward Johnny. The force was enough it grazed his cut that Phoebus previously gave him, which forced Johnny to release his grip on the weapons.

Jake was then swift enough to run past Johnny and catch the blade before it hit the ground. Johnny turned and continued after Jake, but Dash ran in. He swung at Johnny with his batons, non-stop, which forced Johnny to have continuously stepped back and back, and dodged each one, and that allowed zero time to have countered.

Dash then laid in some vicious kicks on Johnny, which forced him back down to the ground. Johnny tried to do the same, but Dash countered them and knocked him back down on the ground.

What's with this guy? I can't seem to find a weakness, not a single one. I should have been doing that while they were talking as opposed to making fun of them. His attacks are relentless! I shouldn't expect anything less from someone who studies in the way of the Tiger.

Dash kicked Johnny in the stomach and Johnny fell down and clutched his stomach, then his rib cage.

"Oh, so Richard did manage to do something after all?" remarked Dash

Wait, can it be?

Jake ran over and kicked Johnny in the rib cage and Dash kicked Johnny in the face. Johnny grabbed Jake's foot and twisted him off, and as Dash went in for another kick, Johnny swept him at the leg.

"I noticed the shift in your leg, you have the slightest limp."

Jake spun and kicked Johnny in the back of his leg which just missed his knee cap. Johnny rose, his adrenaline fully kicked in.

"Jake! Back!" said Anthony.

Jake did a flip back as Anthony darted in. He used this blade attached to his arm to take swipes at Johnny and eventually cut him on the chest in the same exact spot Phoebus cut him earlier.

They keep getting me in the same spot! First Phoebus, then Richard, now them. Nothing is going to hold me back, though!

Johnny did a back flip and fell down on one knee. He desperately tried to catch his breath and looked down at the bleeding, he fell back. Anthony rushed at him and hoped to get his strike in, but Anthony was caught off guard when Johnny did a sideways spin and kicked Anthony's leg and he fell.

They both slowly rose, and firmly placed their feet on the grassy ground below. They squared off in their respective stances. Since Anthony studied in the A.C.P.F., he did a stance similar to Johnny's way of the Black Dragon, only instead of his fingers being extended, they were tucked into fists.

Anthony approached Johnny and punched him in the face, and he stumbled back. Anthony then threw a back fist to Johnny's face successfully, while Johnny tried to punch Anthony. He dodged the attack, so next Johnny tried to kick him, but he dropped down and swept Johnny, and he fell. Johnny rose back up and kicked but before any successful attack happened, Anthony kicked him across the face. Johnny faltered backward, then took one strong step forward.

He extended out his arms and swung them in toward Anthony's ears, slapped them hard, and discombobulated him for a moment, as his ears rang. He then swept him. Johnny turned to see what the others were doing and as he did, he got bumped in the elbow by one of Dash's batons.

Johnny grunted as pins and needles coursed down from his elbow all the way to his fingertips. Dash took another swing at Johnny, but he dropped down and punched Dash right in the kneecap, he then stood up and kicked that kneecap, and Dash fell flat on his face.

Johnny picked up both of Dash's batons and made a move for Dash, but as he did, Dash reached up and grabbed a hold of the batons, then pulled Johnny down, and kneed him in the stomach, which forced Johnny to have released his grip on the batons.

Dash was about to lay a finishing blow to Johnny's head, but he stopped cold. He holstered his batons then stepped back from Johnny.

There was a blinding light that pierced through the canopy—the same light that shone when Simon exhaled his final breath. Dash stared at this light, and in turn so too did Johnny, but what he saw was different than Dash.

"Two overlapping 'M's!" exclaimed Dash, with hint of fear in his eyes.

"Two overlapping 'M's? Is that what that light is?"

"You've seen it before?" asked Dash.

"Only on the way here, but it was faint. Very faint," said Johnny, cautiously.

"This is not the last time you'll see me, kid. I'll be back and stronger than ever," said Dash.

Dash proceeded to run away through the forest and was soon hidden by the trees. As he watched Dash dart into the forest and could no longer make him out, Anthony went in for a kick, but Johnny caught his foot.

He adjusted his grip to be farther up his shin and wrapped his arms tightly around his legs. He then spun down inward toward the ground, and as he did there was a loud cracking sound from Anthony's hip.

Anthony let out a long and shrill scream. So shrill that it could be compared to the bell ting heard earlier, which meant that Anthony's scream escaped the Forest Region.

Jake rushed at Johnny and delivered a swift blow to the face with his left foot, which knocked him back.

"You're nothing but a fool, man. You think you're all high and mighty coming here trying to take down Valmont? The way I see it, you're lucky that Dash ran off and Anthony's hip is injured," commented Jake.

"Luck has nothing to do with it, just skill," replied Johnny.

"Then how about we finish it?"

"How about we just end it right here. Go tend to your brother," said Johnny.

Jake stared long and hard at Johnny before he nodded his head. Johnny nodded his head and as he began turning away, Jake took the blunt end of his blade and forcefully slammed it down onto Johnny's shoulder, which temporarily immobilized Johnny's arm. Jake then punched Johnny and shoved him back. Jake turned and ran toward Anthony.

"What're we going to do?" asked Jake.

"We have to set it," said Anthony.

"Wouldn't that break it even more?" asked Jake.

"No. He's right, it needs to be set," said Johnny.

"Listen, you aren't that skilled. Once again it comes down to luck. If I didn't have to tend to my brother, I'd be defeating you. Just get out of here!" shouted Jake.

"I've had enough of this! Why are you all sticking up for Valmont? Wanting to be his sentries?"

"That's none of your business," said Jake.

"Well, I think it is. I would like to know. Phoebus told me he doesn't much care for Valmont, but that this job pays well. I can understand loathing a job but sticking around for the money, but why Valmont?"

"Phoebus lost his whole family to the war, all right? He has no one else . . . He sought out friends and has a coterie among us sentries here," said Anthony.

"How long have you all been here?" asked Johnny.

"Long enough to know that someone like you . . . you're going to do it. You're going to defeat Valmont. I can see it in your eyes. What's your name?" asked Anthony.

"Johnny Hunderson."

"All of that talk before . . . I just can't believe that a Hunderson came through here. Last time I had seen a Hunderson was when I was deployed. I was good friends with your brothers Hunter and Alex."

"So you *do* know them?" asked Johnny.

"Yes, very well. For what little time they got to spend with you, they spoke a great deal about you. I didn't think I'd ever be fighting you."

"This guy is a Hunderson?" asked Jake.

"Yes, Jake. We shouldn't be fighting like this . . . The Rendars and the Hundersons should be on the same side," said Anthony.

"Try telling that to your brother," said Johnny.

"Which one? Richard or Dash?" asked Anthony, faintly laughing.

"Both of them," he said letting out a laugh.

"What will you do now?" asked Jake.

"While I would much enjoy continuing on this conversation, I cannot linger any longer. I must continue on toward Valmont," said Johnny.

"Johnny, wait. If you really want to defeat all of the evil in this world, then you will need help," said Jake.

"That's what my younger brother Billy keeps telling me," said Johnny.

"Well it's true. There are far greater evils out in Direfell than Valmont."

"So, you'll join me then, Jake? And you, too, Anthony?"

"We can't right now. We're doing this job for the money because, like you, we're in search of our father. We know he's out there somewhere, but he disappeared many waves ago, just like yours," said Jake.

"And you know he's still alive?" asked Johnny.

"He has to be. He's in hiding from some stirring evil, but I just know that when the time is right, he'll come back and defeat the evil once again," said Jake.

"*Once again?* You saying he's defeated evil before?"

"Yes. Back when he was around your age, he went off with a group of friends, similar in skill to his. That is when he formed the Special Snake Service—a service dedicated to helping others and saving them from any evil pillaging their land," said Jake.

"I wonder . . ."

"What?" asked Jake.

"I wonder if your father and my father ever teamed up. I mean, they were both out and around the same time helping others," said Johnny.

"It's a possibility," said Anthony, "After all, if it weren't for your brother saving me, I'd have not been here today."

"Who saved you? Hunter or Alex?"

"Neither of them. We were in different platoons, but we had to squad up on one particular mission. In fact, this was my last mission I did before taking leave to come here with my brothers."

"This mission, where was it?" asked Johnny.

"The Sand Region."

Johnny stared in bewilderment.

"Then it was Derex that saved you?!"

"Yes. He's the one who told me to go on with the others and lead them. He offered to stay back. Have you had contact with him? Is he still alive?"

"No . . . he's dead. I ran into him when leaving my home to come here and I didn't even recognize him," said Johnny.

"What did he say?"

"He kept talking about some approaching shadow—some being that couldn't be beaten."

"An approaching shadow, eh? Look, Johnny, whether Valmont killed your father or not, I don't know, but I'll tell you this . . . Not everything is as it seems. Proceed with caution."

"I hope you'll both join me someday and we can bring down this evil, whatever it might be," said Johnny, "By the way, I was wonder, your sword . . . it's blade is navy-blue. Wherever did you find something like that?"

"I didn't find it, I crafted it on one of my missions far off in the Water Region," said Anthony, with a smile in his tone.

"The Water Region. I remember seeing that on my map," said Johnny, excitedly.

"You have a map of there?"

"Of all of Direfell."

"Where did you ever precure something like that?" asked Anthony.

"From my father's room . . . I grabbed it before leaving to come here. I figured it might help. Sadly, it doesn't detail this place at all otherwise I'd have better prepared for the Forest Region."

"Well, like we said, there haven't always been sentries here. Maybe the map is older. Nevertheless, may I see?" asked Anthony.

"Sure."

Johnny walked over and retrieved his bag, he then headed to both Anthony and Jake. He pulled out the map and showed them. All three of them examined it.

"Wow, this is outdated," said Jake.

"How many waves?" asked Johnny, scratching his head.

"Well, all I can say is the Twilight Region isn't that small. Don't get me wrong, in comparison to this region, it's incredibly small just . . . not that small," commented Anthony, as he ran his finger across the map, showing Johnny the whole expanse of the Twilight Region.

"Interesting. Listen, I need to get going, but when we meet again, I do hope things will be different," said Johnny.

"They will be," said Anthony, "This fight here today was a mistake."

Johnny turned around and headed onward.

"Johnny!" shouted Jake, running up to him.

Jake handed him a small bit of a folded leaf with a hard, circular object inside.

"Until we meet again," said Jake.

Johnny nodded at both Anthony and Jake, then headed on toward the depths of the Forest Region, opposite to the path which Dash ran. After having walked for a few hours now, he reached the edge of a cliff.

This will be the perfect spot to rest up! There's an abundance of sap here, too.

He let curiosity get the better of him and Johnny inched closer to the edge so he could have seen how far down it went. As he did, the cliff crumbled beneath his boots and Johnny fell down, slid, rolled, and shifted down the montane hillside.

When Johnny neared the bottom, he passed through a wall of bushes, which made his otherwise hard impact slightly softer. Despite the bedding like structure of the bushes, Johnny's motion did not stop. He slid through the bushes, off another cliff and descended into water and splashed down hard.

The water carried Johnny's body down the stream that headed west. When Johnny came to, he reached his hands up and grabbed hold of a tree root that extended out into the water. The water forcefully tried to pull Johnny down its stream, but he swung his leg around the root and pulled himself up on top of it.

When he looked up to the canopy, it appeared even higher than before, almost like he descended from the attic of a house all the way down to the basement. Johnny gently climbed down off the tree root and began exploring. He walked straight and noticed something he did not expect. The trees around him began to thin out and for the first time, Johnny saw light—a real light.

Johnny moved closer to the light to examine it more. He reached out his hand blindly like one does when reaching for a towel after getting soap in their eye. He reached the end of the Forest Region, but not the end he sought.

He was on the West End of Direfell; a place to which he had never been before. He moved farther away from the Forest Region, focused on this one piece of snow that gleamed and shimmered, that fell from the sky, which seemed an interminable distance away from where he was currently stood. Johnny then stopped his movement.

I'm being drawn to this almost like it's calling my name. What is it?

"Hello, Johnny."

Johnny turned around and saw a blinding light.

"You don't know me, but I know you all too well."

"Who are you?" asked Johnny.

"So direct. Just like a Hunderson. Listen, I don't have much time, but there is something I need to tell you, or rather, teach you. You've seen this once before, in your dreams. And because of this, you know what must be done."

"I don't understand."

"In time you will. For now, this is all I can give you . . . Continue on, Johnny, you're so close to learning the truth about your father."

"My father. What about him?!"

"All the answers lie beyond this illusion. You can't actually think you fell so far down that you actually reached the West End of the world, now did you? You're still well within the depths of the Forest Region, but I needed an illusion for you to follow so I could speak with you."

"Who are you? Tell me!"

"I am the end of all things. I am the answer. I am the solution. I am what others fear and I am what will return."

"Return?"

"Yes, soon enough, I shall be back. Now go, Johnny. Valmont is just up ahead."

"Up ahead? Where?"

Johnny heard a loud cracking noise. He turned to the direction from which the noise came. It was a tree that fell before him. Johnny dove out of the way, hit his elbow into his rib cage and caused immense pressure on it as he rolled to the ground.

Johnny got up and ached in pain, and saw another pathway formed from this falling tree. As he rose, he looked to where the blinding light was and saw nothing. He heard no voices, nothing around him at all. Whatever illusion or trance he was in was now over as he was still in the depths of the Forest Region. The canopy's height was back to what it was before Johnny's fall.

Was that all an illusion? It can't have been. The tree still fell and is still here. But my fall . . . Did I actually fall off that cliff? What is going on here? This place just gets stranger and stranger.

 *Chapter 18*

Johnny clutched his rib cage and took this new path. It led him to a pond. Johnny knelt and splashed some water on his face and drank some. He looked ahead and when he did, he slowly took out the rolled-up leaf which Jake Rendar gave him and placed the whole thing in his mouth. He then drank more water and pulled out the leaf from his mouth having swallowed the contents that had been wrapped inside.

He stood up and looked at his reflection. He pulled back the wrappings a little and saw his wounds which have finally stopped their bleeding. He then looked in front of him and saw four silhouettes.

The grass was so high here it would probably be up to his waist. The trees retreated here, which allowed for more of an open view, much like the other open grass areas. This area was not as bright, or faux-bright as the other areas in which Johnny had been. There was a calmness to the forest—not a single element moving as it stood or rested perfectly still.

There was absolute silence, until a figure tinged a bell. This bell's ring was so shrill and sharp that if it were a source of wind, it would have torn down these trees. Johnny stood on his tiptoes trying to get a better view of the four silhouettes. He heard a voice from one of them.

"We've been waiting for you, Johnny. We didn't know you'd take this long. Enjoy the water?" asked a voice from the depths.

Great, a wise guy.

"How do you plan on beating us? We are the Elected Four, Valmont's personal bodyguards. If you thought the others were tough, wait until you see what we're capable of," said the same voice as before.

Why does everyone feel the need to introduce themselves?

Johnny looked at the four silhouettes and tried to see which was talking. He could barely make out what they looked like. Johnny continued forward.

"Well, if it isn't the infamous John Hunderson, Junior. Yes, we know all about you," said the same voice.

He must have been the one talking. He's standing to the immediate right which implies leadership if it's an even number of people.

"I am Michael Oasis, but much like you, I, too, go by a nickname. Mikey. I am the strongest of the Elected Four."

Johnny looked over to his right and tried to get a better view of Mikey.

His attire was composed of dark gray long sleeved under armor, with dark gray under armor pants that matched. Over his dark gray long sleeve under armor was a sage green colored tunic with shoulder pads. Around his waist was a black belt, wrapped around so no strings were hung down. With this he wore sage green pants over his dark gray under armor pants which tucked into his brown combat boots. This attire gave him the ability to blend in more with the Forest Region, much like Phoebus'.

"I am Mikey's brother, Leo Oasis."

"I can see, you're dressed almost identically. Get a discount?"

asked Johnny, sarcastically.

The difference in Leo's attire was that it was forest green, instead of sage green. With this, he also had metal guarders on each of his forearms, extending from his elbow down to the wrist. These guarders did not hinder his ability to bend his arms, though. Similarly, he also had metal half-greaves around his legs. These extended from right above his kneecaps down to his ankles. He wore his brown boots over his leg guarders as an extra layer of protection. His vambraces were of a silver color and were used to deflect and parry weapons and projectiles, such as arrows and swords.

"I am Freddy Ydderf."

Those trappings are unlike any I've ever seen before.

Freddy was dressed in different colored trappings, mostly of a brown and sandy color. This was due to him hailing from the Sand Region. He had a sandy brown bandana tied around his head, and the shirt he wore had such long sleeves that it covered his hands, with four strands of string that hung off each sleeve. His attire was similar to Mikey and Leo's, but the color was different. Freddy wore brown boots with a circular disk around his calves; this is for when he travelled through the sand as to not let any in. His sandy brown pants were tucked into his boots.

"I am Jonas Rex, but everyone calls me Rhino Rex, Rhino, or just Rex."

I can see why; this guy is huge! He's incredibly muscular and so defined.

He was dressed in camouflage pants with brown boots. He also wore a white muscle shirt, and a red hat.

"Why the hat? You're dressed so differently from the others," said Johnny.

"I'm a street fighter, that's why. I'll use my hat to attack my opponents by flinging it hard at their faces, or using it to catch an attack, like a punch. Then I'll close the hat on their hand and flip them over," stated Rhino Rex.

"Why're you telling me how you fight?" asked Johnny.

"It really doesn't matter what I tell you. This is where your adventure ends," said Rhino Rex.

These are some outfits these guys have on. And that one, all the way to the left . . . Did he fill his arms with rocks? His biceps are insanely huge!

Mikey stood tall before Johnny and stared at him. Johnny inched closer and Mikey brushed his hair out from over his face which revealed his yellow eyes, that glowed.

"I didn't think you existed," said Johnny.

"What is that now?" asked Mikey.

"In my research, I heard about you, or people like you," said Johnny.

"Oh, did you now?" asked Mikey.

"Yes. The Enchanted Eye Entities. That must be what the colors meant . . . Unique people in the world with unique eye colors. Here I was thinking people like you didn't exist at all."

"Are you that much of a dimwit that you didn't even notice your own cousin's eye color?" asked Mikey.

"What do you mean?"

"Wallace, you fool. He has purple eyes . . . He's one of us. He is a beast as well."

"He—no. Wallace?"

He was wearing something to cover his eyes when I bumped into him. What Ryan was saying must be true.

"Yes. Wallace Ecallaw."

"It's so strange to think that there are beasts like you roaming this land," said Johnny.

"Even stranger to think how ignorant you are to the rest of the world and even more so strange that you're still alive!"

I've got to face all four of these guys and I've had little time to rest since my fight with the Rendar brothers.

"Your time is up, child. I hope you're ready to die, because there is no way you're going to make it past us," said Mikey.

Trying to stay strong, Johnny said, "We'll see about that, punk."

Rhino Rex, the man who stood all the way to the left, ran at Johnny and kicked him right in the mouth. Johnny dropped to the grassy ground and coughed up a bit of blood.

"How'd that feel, kid?" asked Rhino Rex, "You want some more? Just keep on getting up, I'll show you."

What am I going to do about him?

Johnny bled and had relentlessly been kicked in the mouth numerous times. He attempted to get back up and as he did, Rhino Rex kneed him in the face and knocked him back down. Johnny started to move his head side to side to avoid being kicked in the face by him.

Coughing, Johnny said, "I'm not going to give up ever. I've come all this way and I'm not going to be beaten by someone like you."

Johnny kept getting stomped on by Rhino Rex, which crushed his chest, yet Johnny could not seem to break free.

He rolled out of the way to avoid some of his stomping, but it couldn't be continued, as his chest hurt too much. He watched Rhino Rex's foot and counted the time of impact to the time he lifted up his foot, this allowed him to roll away.

Rhino Rex lifted Johnny by his tunic which ripped it even more as he did. Johnny's Black Dragon's foot tattoo was now clearly visible. Rhino Rex headbutted Johnny then slammed him down to the ground and this caused a loud thump as he landed on his back.

As Rhino Rex went to stomp on Johnny, he caught his foot and pushed it up, then swept his other foot and knocked him backward, which caused Rhino Rex to fix his stance. Johnny, who was still feeling the blood course down his face, rose.

He uppercut Rhino Rex right to his chin and this move knocked him on his back. Johnny started to stomp on his face. And after the first stomp, he knocked him out. Freddy immediately tackled Johnny off him.

"You think you can stomp someone's face, kid?" asked Freddy, "Well, you're dead wrong."

"It only seemed fair, after all the punches I just took," said Johnny.

"Well, I'll try to fix that problem for 'ya, kid," said Freddy.

Freddy went to punch Johnny and connected his fist with his face, turning Johnny's face to the right. Freddy then did a flying kick into Johnny's stomach. Freddy continued to do some foot maneuvers on Johnny, which meant he swung his foot in direction which he turned his body for more of an impactful attack. With each attack, Freddy was successful.

Freddy kicked Johnny so hard that it knocked him back and Freddy ran over to him and continuously slammed his fists upon Johnny's face until he managed to monkey flip Freddy off him. Freddy got up quickly, but Johnny just laid there. Freddy walked over to him.

"What's with that tattoo on your upper right chest? Go back to where you came from."

"This tattoo is a symbol that all Hundersons have. It signifies that we are one," stated Johnny, coughing.

"You're done, kid. You're a waste of time!"

"Don't ever count me out!" shouted Johnny.

Johnny kicked Freddy's kneecap and as he did there was a loud popping sound. Freddy's kneecap buckled, which caused him to collapse. He shouted in agony. Johnny rolled over and slowly got up and clenched his rib cage.

Johnny turned to face Leo and he just stared at him, then slowly walked toward him and eventually charged at him and screamed.

"You're crazy! You just got attacked multiple times, no way you're going to land a successful attack," said Leo.

Leo prepared for a counterattack and kneed Johnny right in his diaphragm and threw him back. Johnny fell to one knee, but soon rose and ran at Leo again. Leo jumped to the side. He then dropped to his side extended his legs and swept Johnny down to the ground. Leo got up, lifted Johnny and threw him back. Johnny could not get up and just laid there hoping for a chance to have healed. Leo, however, walked toward him.

"You're finished," said Leo.

Leo raised his leg and aimed to stomp on Johnny until he died. Out of nowhere an arrow was shot down at Leo, but he lifted his left arm and deflected the arrow with his vambrace.

"You may know nothing of me, but I know we fight to bring down the same man," said a voice from the trees.

Valmont, who was sitting in his stone chair, glanced up at the trees.

"A traitor, eh?" said Valmont, quietly.

As he coughed profusely, Johnny raised his head to see Phoebus who was in the trees.

"This is my fight and mine alone!" Johnny screamed.

Johnny got up and stumbled back. Leo swung his leg to the right at Johnny, but he ducked down to evade it. However, Leo brought his foot back across to the left and hit Johnny right in the face and knocked him down.

Leo went to kick him in the face again. Johnny caught his leg, then threw it down. Phoebus, who saw that Johnny was not rising, continually shot arrows at Leo, which distracted him and made him parry them off with his vambraces while he backed up.

Leo ran toward the trees and made his way for Phoebus. As he did, Johnny rose slowly and hit Leo right in the throat which made him gasp for air. Johnny then grabbed ahold of his neck and choked him out which took a matter of mere seconds now. They both dropped to their knees and Leo blacked out.

Meanwhile, Mikey ran at both of them. He shouldered Johnny off his brother, then grabbed Johnny, faced him the other way and threw him face down to the ground. Mikey then jumped on Johnny's back and put him in a chokehold similar to that of the hold which Johnny had Leo in. Johnny could not get up or break free, no matter how much he tried.

"What're you going to do now, Johnny?" asked Mikey, "How do you plan on getting up and striking me?"

Johnny could not breathe but looked up with blurred vision.

That man, in the chair, it's him, it's Valmont. I can't make him out, but it has to be him. I can't fail now; I've come too far and fought too hard to lose it all here and now. To die here would be worthless after coming all this way and going to all lengths. No!

"Ah yes, that's Valmont you see in that chair. Too bad you won't get your shot at facing him. You've come all this way only to fail now," said Mikey.

As Mikey was distracted by grandstanding, Johnny took two fingers and jabbed them sharply at Mikey's wrist, which sent a jolting shock up Mikey's arm and caused his grip to be released. Johnny tried to get up but could only get to his knees before Mikey was able to gain control of Johnny once more and choked him again.

"Smart move, using the nervous system. Too bad you won't do something like that again," said Mikey, tightening his grip around Johnny's neck.

Johnny began to lose feeling in his arms from the immense amount of pressure Mikey applied.

There isn't much time left . . . Another ten or so seconds and I'll blackout.

Johnny wiggled his body, he then forcefully swung his legs out in front of himself. He twisted out of Mikey's grasp of his neck, then bumped Mikey back. Johnny, desperately caught his breath, slowly rose and assumed his stance in the way of the Black Dragon, while Mikey assumed his stance in a similar pose.

"No way! How do you know this style?"

"Come now, Johnny. Your father first taught his family then made his teachings all over Direfell. I learned from him and his subordinates in these classes," said Mikey.

"It doesn't matter since you're not a Hunderson. You'll never be as good as I am. You're not a true master in the way of the Black Dragon," said Johnny, confidently.

"From what I hear, neither are you. Your dad left before completing your training huh?" said Mikey, taunting the young man before him.

The two stared at one another and assessed each other before making any sudden movements. Mikey charged at Johnny then threw a successful punch to his face. Mikey then proceeded with a hay-maker, but Johnny blocked this attack with his forearm. Mikey aimed a kick for Johnny's rib cage, but Johnny blocked by having dropped down his arm to guard.

The force of Mikey's kick was still strong enough to cause Johnny some pain. After a few more unsuccessful punches were thrown, Mikey ceased his fighting.

"I really wish you were at your best so I could face you at your fullest potential," said Mikey.

"Showing compassion while on the battlefield?" asked Johnny.

"No, all I'm saying is I wish I could fight you at your full potential, but you're so badly beaten up, I'll not get that chance . . . Not today anyway."

"Gonna be hard to fight me again after I maim you into oblivion, Mikey."

"There it is, that winning Hunderson personality," said Mikey, sarcastically.

"What's that supposed to mean?" asked Johnny.

"I'm not a killer, I'm not a killer," said Mikey, mockingly, "Too bad that can't be said since you killed Simon."

"That was his doing, not mine. The only life I will be taking today is Valmont's. A life for a life," said Johnny.

"Regardless, I won't be the maimed one, Johnny. Not I."

Johnny pressed hard on his rib, which put it into a state where he felt no pain from it.

"'Ya know, fixing it like that won't make it any better," stated Mikey. "One swift kick to your rib cage again and it's broken . . . permanently. Then again, if I had kicked it in any farther, you would have died. Either way, your rib cage is gone."

"You're a smart guy, aren't you?"

"I like to crack jokes . . . and ribs," replied Mikey in a mischievous tone.

"I'm done talking with you; we finish this thing right now!"

"Have it your way," replied Mikey.

Johnny and Mikey, once again, squared off in their respective stances. This time, Mikey's stance was that of the way of the Tiger.

"You know more than one way of fighting?" asked Johnny.

"Most everyone in the world does, Johnny. You never know what enemies you'll be facing; you have to be prepared," said Mikey.

"It doesn't matter how many fighting styles you know; I won't lose to you."

"That's a slippery slope, Johnny, but you'd know all about that, right?"

Johnny took a swing at Mikey, but Mikey caught his arm, then wrapped his other arm around it and dropped down to the ground and flipped Johnny way over him.

They both rose back up. Mikey ran at Johnny, but he countered by a quick sweep, which knocked him down to the ground. Once again, they both rose and faced off against one another.

As they both charged, this time they each performed a flying kick toward each other, but since they both did the same move, they cancelled each other out and both pushed off each other's foot and jumped back.

Johnny ran at Mikey and went to kick him, so he lifted his leg and blocked Johnny's kick. Mikey then punched Johnny down to the ground, but he rose and threw a back fist to him successfully.

They both squared off again and Mikey threw a successful straight punch, then another. He then swung his elbow across Johnny's face, then swung it upward, and uppercut him. Mikey slammed his elbow down on his face and kicked him back.

Mikey rushed at Johnny with a fist and went to punch, but he countered and threw him over his shoulder, so Mikey rose and again did the same thing, so once more Johnny performed the same counter and threw him over his shoulder.

Johnny ran at Mikey and went to kick him, but he blocked this kick and again lifted his leg. He then rolled under Johnny and swept him down to his knees. Mikey choked him again, like he had done earlier.

"Not here. Not today," said Johnny.

"What are you murmuring about, Johnny? I can barely hear you over your choking!"

Johnny this time grabbed Mikey's legs, jumped up to his feet, then jumped up and slammed Mikey on the ground which created a loud thud as pieces of dirt and grass flew up.

Johnny gave Mikey some back elbows to each side of his rib cage. Mikey blinked numerous times and gasped for air. Johnny got up and Mikey looked up at him.

"I told you, nothing is going to stop me," Johnny said in a raspy voice, "I've come too far."

"How?"

"Earlier, when at the pond drinking water . . . I took a special pill. This pill was given to me by a friend to increase my resistance to attacks. Like I said . . . for you, it's all over."

Johnny slammed his foot right on Mikey's face and knocked him out. Johnny turned slowly and faced Valmont.

"Okay, Valmont, give me all you got, I'm ready."

Letting out a menacing laugh Valmont replied: "You're not ready. You barely survived that last fight. Come to think of it, you've barely survived any fight you've been placed up against. You're not ready for what I'm prepared to do to you; you're going to receive a little taste of death today, Johnny Hunderson. Then you're going to experience it!"

"I'm ready for anything you can throw at me!"

Valmont lunged out from the shadowy covering of his stone chair and punched Johnny who fell to the ground. Johnny looked up at Valmont who stood tall, in his dark gray body suit that tightly hugged his muscles, underneath his dark gray tunic.

His gray mask covered to just above his mouth. On his left shoulder was a large, metal pauldron. This particular pauldron was used to block attacks of all forms, even able to have withstood the broadest of sword strokes.

Valmont also had a blade attachment on his right forearm, much like Anthony's, only Valmont's had four spiked blades attached to it. Down his thigh on the right was a pouch strapped around his leg that contained a blade. Beneath this blade were his combat boots, in their black color. These boots had clasps on both ends and were very blunt.

Almost like mini batons attached to them. Johnny shivered in a panic, and slowly looked up at the figure before him.

"You have no idea what you've gotten yourself into, Johnny."

Chapter 19

Valmont towered over Johnny and peered down at him as he laid down on the ground, unable to have gotten up. Behind Valmont he saw a stone chair. On its right was a shield, with a crest embossed on it. This was the same shield from before. Its pristine condition still held true. The sword to the left of the stone chair was different than any other sword crafted before.

Valmont stepped back to the stone chair and picked up the sword, he swirled it around which created a sharp whooshing noise. Valmont looked up and saw a leaf that fell from one of the trees, so he twirled the sword once in his hand then sliced at the leaf and cut it perfectly in half. He then flung the leaf up back into the sky from the tip of his sword, then sliced the leaf into many tiny pieces, which all glided on down and each one landed in front of Johnny's feet.

"Do you know where I got this sword, Johnny? Of course not. You've probably never even heard of this place, or maybe you saw it on a map once. Either way, allow me to enlighten you . . ."

Johnny looked at the sword Valmont was grasping in his hands. This sword had an onyx hue to the hilt and its blade was extremely long and sharp, like an overgrown branch that extended from a tree. The color of the blade was a fiery red-orange color.

"You may be wondering where a sword gets a blade of this color.

This due to the sword being crafted in the Fire Region. You see, there was once a time when swords were the weapon of craft and many crafters would make their blades from the finest materials in the world. This sword was made from the lava of Firetop Rock—an active volcano deep in the beyond of the Fire Region, far past the lava sea. A place you won't live to see."

Johnny stared in awe.

"I created this sword under the tutelage of my master . . . You see, unlike you, I'm a master in everything I've studied. Despite the waves of age I have on you, that means nothing," said Valmont.

"It doesn't matter. You're a murderer! A person like you only masters things through the fear of others!"

"Come now, Johnny, surely you know that fear has nothing to do with it."

His muscles, he's . . . he's so muscular. Phoebus and Richard weren't kidding. And what's with this mask? What is he hiding, the only visible thing is his mouth and those glowing gray eyes, staring into mine. Dead into mine.

"Ah, I see that mind of yours going to work. You're wondering about my eyes, aren't you? How many unique eye colors am I going to see on my adventure, you must be thinking."

If he's one of those Enchanted Eye Entities then I need to end this fight while he's distracted.

Johnny tried to rise but Valmont again punched Johnny and he stumbled backward and landed on his back. Valmont lifted his foot and Johnny rolled out of the way when Valmont stomped down which left an imprint in the ground.

He then tried to stab down his sword into Johnny, but he rolled out of the way, so Valmont kicked him with his other foot and then stomped on Johnny's chest. Johnny could hardly breathe as he struggled to get up to fight Valmont. He leaned down and lifted Johnny with his hand and grabbed him by what was left of his torn shirt. Valmont's eyes looked at the tattoo on his chest.

He dropped him down, slammed his hilt onto Johnny's shoulders, then stabbed his sword into the ground. He then gave Johnny a right hook, then a left, followed by a back fist and ended with a kick and Johnny was flung back and landed hard on his back.

Johnny was calmly still and tried not to let the pain overcome his body. The pill Jake Rendar gave him slowly began to wear off.

"I'm no fool, Johnny. I know that you were given a pill. You shouted it out for everyone to hear as you delivered a finishing blow to Mikey," said Valmont.

"Then what're you waiting for? Why not just finish me off if you're so strong."

"Its effects were to stimulate the body and put it in a comatose like state—essentially paralyzing the body from any pain."

Johnny laid still.

"While the damage would still be done to the body, its user would not be subject to the pain, until, of course, when the effects wear off. Which should be happening momentarily, since the effects of that particular kind of pill that Jake Rendar carries only last thirty minutes. You tried valiantly to fight off the Elected Four and still have enough of the pill left to fight me, but to no avail. I see all in this Forest Region, Johnny. As well as hear all . . ."

"If you heard everything then why act so surprised at my ability to endure the pain?"

"I heard much more than that . . . You're here to learn about your father, aren't you, boy? Yes, I've heard all about your talks in the Bulwark Bazaar. My sentries are good for more than just fighting. However, you killed one of my better informants and you're going to pay for that"

Johnny was still and made no remark.

"Regardless of if he asked for his death or not, you came into this place innocent, but will now die a killer. As for your father, did you ever think that he is not dead, that there is something bigger going on at hand in Direfell? You're too concerned with someone who is alive and is out there."

Johnny, who just laid completely still, replied: "What do you mean he's alive?"

"I mean just that. Your father John Hunderson Sr. is alive. He was last seen atop a clock tower in Wakesfield matched in a fight with Shadow, the leader of the Mystery Men."

"Who are the Mystery Men?"

"The Mystery Men are a skilled set of people. In fact, Simon was one . . . but he pledged his allegiance to me due to what his leader, Shadow did to him."

Johnny sat up slightly and listened to Valmont.

"What happened?" asked Johnny.

"Simon failed to assassinate me. You see, the Mystery Men and I have this sort of thing where we stay out of each other's way, or so it's supposed to be. I guess Shadow had other plans. He sent one of his supposed best to kill me, but he failed. I spared Simon's life and told him to report to Shadow that I was dead."

"I take it that didn't work out too well then?"

"Correct, Johnny. Simon went back to Shadow to report my death, but somehow Shadow knew . . . His source of information is far greater than I have ever seen in this world."

"He poisoned him, didn't he?" asked Johnny.

"Something to that effect."

"I noticed Simon was coughing a lot, even coughing up a bit of blood at times. Then there was his leg."

"Yes, Simon came back and told me his time would soon be over as Shadow had cast something on him to make his body slowly break down. It's a cruel tactic. Despite his time coming to an end, his body would have broken down over the course of the next three waves. This was the final wave before his life was ending. Despite our best efforts with the Forest Region's healing sap, the very best we could do was a fractured leg and his cough," said Valmont.

"How can someone so skilled be so easily beaten?"

"You know nothing of my skill, Johnny."

"How skilled are the Mystery Men?" asked Johnny.

"So skilled they're almost as legendary as the Feared Five."

"Who are the Feared Five?"

"Honestly, Johnny, do you know anything? The Feared Five were the first to roam this world. They are so skilled; people consider them not human. I know they're real, though, after all, I . . ." he paused and looked back down at Johnny. "You cannot beat them in any style of fighting, they're too great. They know all styles of fighting, all spells, everything! You should really be concerned about the Mystery Men,

Johnny; they pose a great threat to you. Their leader, Shadow, is not one you should trifle with. However, if he ever were to set foot in my Forest Region, he, and his whole squad of shadow ninjas would be destroyed! Be cautious anytime you find yourself near a mystery man, Johnny."

"My father was fighting the leader, Shadow?"

"Yes."

"Why should I be cautious? How will I know if I'm near one?"

"You won't. In fact, rumor is, there's one lurking around the Forest Region somewhere amongst other foul beasts and kind out there."

"Foul beasts? I thought no animals of any kind roamed this region?" asked Johnny.

"Oh they do, just . . . not in this particular area."

"Simon was a Mystery Man wasn't he? If Shadow controls them, then that must be the case."

"Yes, Johnny."

"What was that blinding light that emitted from Simon's body?"

Valmont did not reply.

If what he's saying is true, then I might have seen one, and if they're as good as he said then it's no wonder it disappeared, and I couldn't find it.

"Why are you telling me all of this?" Johnny asked.

"You think I'm the enemy, but you have no idea the truth behind all of this. Everything that has been set into motion cannot be stopped. Believe me or don't, the choice is yours. Much like with what Ryan told you."

"It was you that came to the rooftop?"

"No. I haven't left the Forest Region in almost six waves.

"Six waves? That's right around the time when—"

"You got that pathetic tattoo you so proudly display."

"What do you know of it! This tattoo shows that I'm a Hunderson and I'm proud of it!"

"I know a great deal more than you think, Johnny. Remember, I have eyes and ears everywhere."

Johnny said, slowly rising: "You're a liar, you killed my father and I am going to destroy you!"

Johnny stood up tall, took a deep breath and charged at Valmont.

"This fool really things he can beat me. He's ridiculous, just like his father, always trying to gain the advantage on me," Valmont said to himself.

Johnny gave a kick to Valmont, but Valmont blocked it, then threw Johnny back.

Phoebus who was still high above in the trees watched the fight that ensued. He heard a noise and immediately turned around and drew an arrow strung in his bow.

"Come around too, huh?" asked Phoebus.

Phoebus lowered his bow and put his arrow back in his quiver.

"Yeah, you too, I see. Let's move."

"No," said Phoebus.

"Why not?"

"He doesn't want our help; this is something he must do alone."

The two of them stood there and watched as Johnny desperately tried to best Valmont. After he had been flung back, Johnny again rose.

"You won't stop me! I'm going to destroy you!"

Johnny charged at Valmont and did a flying kick toward him. Valmont caught his foot, but Johnny flipped and punched him right in his stomach. Johnny dropped and gave Valmont a swift kick to the back of the knee.

Valmont fell down, then rose. Johnny continuously did the same kick until Valmont could not get back up. Valmont was knelt and faced Johnny who struggled very much as he searched for air and stumbled.

Mikey along with Leo came around and got up and they both charged at Johnny.

"Look at them, pathetic, they think they're going to make it to Johnny," said Phoebus.

An arrow shot from Phoebus went and grazed Mikey's leg which brought him down. Phoebus attempted to do the same to Leo, but the arrow careened off the man's half-greaves, harmless.

The man who stood next to Phoebus dropped down from the trees, used his weapon to glide down along the tree's trunk and scraped it as the bark flew everywhere. He ran at Leo and headed him off and they began to battle. Leo, shocked, no longer ran.

"Richard? What're you doing?" asked Leo.

"I'm my own person now, get used to it."

Richard swung his staff blade at Leo. It clashed against Leo's metal arm and leg guards. They merely parried each other's attacks.

They fought back toward Freddy who rose and went to kick Richard. He was now faced with Leo and Freddy. Richard swept Freddy who trembled for a moment, so Richard kicked him in the face and knocked him back down.

"Phoebus, Rex!" yelled Richard, still clashing with Leo.

Phoebus turned toward the tree and stabbed an arrow into it. He attached a rope and slid down it and used one of his daggers and cut it loose once he reached the ground. He then raced down to Rhino

Rex and appeared over him.

"Nice try, bub," said Phoebus with a smile on his face.

Phoebus stomped on Rhino Rex's face which knocked him back out.

Johnny turned around to look only to see Phoebus and Richard who fought off Leo. Johnny turned back to Valmont who cannot rise.

"You're nothing but a liar, you killed my father, and now I'm going to kill you."

Johnny roundhouse kicked Valmont to the face.

Looks like my adrenaline is kicking in.

A stray arrow from Phoebus flew past Johnny and grazed the top of Valmont's tunic, which caused a slight tear. Johnny grabbed Valmont with two hands and struggled to lift him up. A stretching and ripping noise was heard from Valmont's armor as Johnny raised Valmont up even higher.

Valmont stood and shoved Johnny back. He then walked at Johnny and threw punches, but he missed, which was not like Valmont.

"Off your balance, Valmont?"

"You fool, look what's directly in front of you."

Johnny saw that Valmont purposefully missed so he could get back to where his sword was stabbed in the ground. With one fell swoop, Valmont grabbed his sword from the grassy ground and pulled it out. He swung the sword at Johnny, but he flipped backwards, which caused Valmont to have sliced through the grass. This caused detached blades of green to float in the air before being struck back down as Valmont swung another hacking swing at Johnny.

This is it!

Johnny knelt down and clasped his hands together and successfully stopped Valmont's attack. Shocked, Valmont quickly pulled back his sword which cut Johnny's hands slightly. Johnny placed his hand over his Black Dragon's foot tattoo.

Valmont watched in awe as Johnny performed this move. This move seemed to distract everyone; it halted all the ongoing fighting. Everyone was fixated on Johnny and watched as he closed his eyes and inhaled once, then exhaled slowly.

"Enough of this. Your time is up, Johnny!'

Valmont sliced down toward Johnny with a killing stroke, but Johnny rolled onto his back, extended up one foot, and kicked the hilt of Valmont's sword which knocked it into the air. Johnny rose to his feet, kicked Valmont back, then caught his sword and did a spinning swing, that sliced Valmont across his tunic, which made a large tear across the whole top area.

Johnny stabbed the sword into the ground then does a flying kick and Valmont was flown back into his stone chair, which caused it to crack.

Valmont slowly raised his head, then clutched his knee and looked at Johnny. Johnny walked up to Valmont.

Each footstep brought Johnny closer to his enemy—the blades of grass were now waist high as Johnny neared Valmont's stone chair. They caressed his body, wrapped themselves around his hips, then gently released from his legs, almost as if they were pushing him to his victory.

As Johnny got closer to Valmont, he looked more carefully at where his tunic is torn. He noticed a large slash mark from where he successfully sliced across his chest and watched as the blood dripped down slowly. This, however, was not what caught Johnny's eye. His eyes instead shifted to a particular part of Valmont's torn tunic, in the upper right, that revealed a tattoo. Johnny stopped dead in his tracks.

Chapter 20

Johnny was frozen, unable to move from a strain on his body from the mass amount of stress he just received from his brain's signals to his body. A solid state of paralysis. All the forces in the world could not bring Johnny to move.

Johnny was shut off from the rest of the world; he did not even notice that the others have returned to fighting. He no longer heard the clashing of Richard's staff blade as it hit against Leo's metal guarders. He no longer heard Phoebus' daggers when they twirled around as they tried to strike Leo. He heard nothing but the sound of his heartbeat which got faster.

His heart pounded harder and harder, and Johnny felt that if his heart were to pound any harder, it would beat right out of his chest and he'd have seen his very own heart in front of him, on the grassy ground beneath his very feet. This was no illusion. This was no dream. Everything Johnny saw and felt was absolutely real.

The same Black Dragon's foot, but if he has that tattoo . . .

"Confused, Johnny? Shocked to see this Black Dragon's foot tattoo on me? Makes you wonder who I am; what connection I have to you and your whole wretched family, doesn't it?"

Johnny just continued to stare at Valmont; his body began to rain sweat which flooded him in a watery mess. His eyes peeled open wide as one might have done if they tried to see in the dark. Johnny's whole body had left its paralyzed state and shivered and shook.

"You idiot, haven't you figured it out yet? The tattoo, my style of fighting; how I know so much about your father. Didn't he ever tell you about me before he took off and left you and the rest of your brothers? No, he's only told you about Dumont."

Johnny opened his mouth in attempt to let words escape. His mind raced all around like a person with a shopping list—he could only get out three words.

"Who . . . Are . . . You?"

"I'm your uncle, Johnny."

Johnny stared in utter shock.

"I wonder if John kept Andrew a secret, too," said Valmont to himself.

Valmont looked past Johnny at a figured that approached.

This figure rushed into the open grass area and sprinted past an unconscious Mikey and Rhino Rex. It scurried past a barely conscious Freddy and made its way toward Johnny.

Leo saw this and attempted to get away from Richard and Phoebus to make for the figure, but Richard whacked him across the face with the other end of his staff and Phoebus and Richard made their way over to the figure. Johnny turned around.

"Billy?!"

Billy continued to run toward Johnny.

"What's going on here? Who are you people? Who do I even trust?" asked Billy, frantically.

"I told you to wait on the outskirts, Billy. You shouldn't be here," said Johnny.

"Johnny!"

"Billy, stop, don't come any closer."

Valmont pulled out a knife and looked at it, almost as if he had wondered what to do with it.

"Every time I look at you, I see nothing but your father, my brother. I see the failure that happened so many waves ago. I cannot bear this pain anymore," said Valmont.

Johnny turned back to Valmont and stepped closer to him.

"What pain, what are you talking about?"

Valmont grabbed Johnny then quickly jabbed the knife into his body. He pulled out the knife and pushed him back.

"Almost six waves ago, *they* were still roaming Direfell. The madness that ensued and caused this family to spiral into what it is now. The final test," said Valmont.

Johnny dropped down to his knees, grabbed his stab wound, and tried to suppress it as it bled.

"Johnny!" shouted Billy.

"It's a shame you won't be around to fulfill your journey and end Direfell's cruelty," said Valmont, as he wiped the blood off the knife and placed it back in his pouch.

Billy just stood there, overcame with the same state of paralysis Johnny's body just lived. Phoebus and Richard arrived next to Billy.

"Johnny!" screamed Billy.

"Ha. Pathetic fool, you're . . . noth . . . ing," said Valmont as his eyes shut.

Billy pushed through Phoebus and Richard as he ran to Johnny and grabbed him. Billy glanced up at Valmont. Phoebus turned around and noticed that Leo had risen back to his feet, as did Freddy. Phoebus and Richard made their way toward Billy.

"Billy. I take it you have some connection with Johnny."

"He's my brother. Who are you two?"

"We don't have time for introductions. We need to get Johnny out of here," said Phoebus.

"Billy, go ahead with Phoebus. I'll finish off what's left of the Elected Four."

Richard spun his blade staff, grasped it and assumed a stance as Mikey, Rhino Rex, Freddy and Leo all got up and charged at him. Phoebus looked at Billy and helped put Johnny over his shoulder.

"Let's go!" said Phoebus.

Phoebus ran with Billy by his side. Billy had Johnny over his shoulder.

"Billy, we're allies. My name is Phoebus. You can trust me," said Phoebus as they made their way out.

Billy turned around to make sure Richard would be all right and instead spotted a figure that ran deep into the forest.

"No way!"

He looked back at Valmont's stone chair and noticed that he was no longer there.

"So, he's not dead then?" asked Billy.

"Valmont? No. He'll be back," said Phoebus.

Billy, Phoebus, and Johnny all made it out of Valmont's base. They ran back through the Forest Region, jumped over trees, and ran through the grass. They passed the open grass area where Jake and Anthony would have been, but they were not there.

"We'll cut through this way, it'll be faster," said Phoebus.

They cut through a path which diverted away from the open grass areas where Valmont's sentries resided.

"We need to stop, Phoebus, he's not going to make it!"

"We're almost to the outskirts."

"How can we almost be there? The Forest Region takes a bit, almost two to travel through."

"When you move straight forward, yes, the Forest Region can take almost two bits, but when you move through the back paths, it's faster."

"Can you take the back paths to reach Valmont's base?"

"No. He set up his base so the only way to get to him is by going through all of his sentries. Although it would appear Johnny found a path that cuts off some sentries as he came directly to me."

Billy stopped running and set Johnny down.

"You mean to tell me you fought him?"

"Yes, Billy. It was my job to protect Valmont."

Billy threw a punch at Phoebus, but he caught it.

"Billy. Listen. We don't have time for this. I'll explain once we reach the outskirts. We must hurry! The other sentries could have been alerted by now."

Billy, in a fit of rage, picked Johnny back up and put him back over his shoulder. Billy and Phoebus continued to run back to the outskirts of the Forest Region. As they made their exit, Billy set Johnny down and immediately tended to his wound. They then heard a noise, so Phoebus quickly drew his bow and strung and arrow to it.

"Again? Stop sneaking up on us, Richard" said Phoebus.

"What happened to the rest of the Elected Four?" asked Billy.

"I took care of them; no need to worry about a thing, Billy."

"Worry about a thing? I don't even know who you two are. For all I know you could be wanting to kill me."

Richard, taken aback by this comment raised his staff blade and went in toward Billy. Phoebus quickly drew a dagger and stopped his staff blade.

"It's just like you Hundersons to instigate something without cause!" shouted Richard.

"Enough. Both of you. If we wanted to kill you, you would be dead. If we wanted to kill you, we wouldn't be helping you," said Phoebus.

"I should have gone with him, none of this should have happened, if I didn't run in on him . . . I had been following him . . . He told me to wait on the outskirts, but I just couldn't. I followed behind him the entire time. It's all my fault."

"Actually, you were following Richard most likely. Once Johnny and I came to an understanding, I allowed him to pass. I went on up ahead to see how he'd fair against Richard, but when I had gotten there, Johnny had already moved on. I noticed Richard was unconscious. I went down to check on him and noticed he has a cut that was tended to."

"Johnny did that?" asked Richard.

"Yes, he spared your life when you wanted his," said Phoebus, "He's not the enemy."

"To me, he is. Anyone who enters this Forest Region is. That's the whole point of this job," said Richard.

"You were smart enough to stay behind and track Richard, figuring that if I got to Richard without any other sentry between us, that it'd be safe to follow him. By this point, Johnny was already well on his way to defeating Simon. It had been at least four days you were behind him," said Phoebus.

"I should have gotten to him sooner. I am still to blame," said Billy.

"Billy, no one is at fault here," said Phoebus, "You didn't know the outcome of the battle; you didn't even know what was inside the Forest Region, let alone Valmont's base on the North End. As far as you could tell, it was just trees and grass as far as the eye could see."

"I guess you're right, Phoebus."

Billy placed Johnny, seated up, in front of a tree and tried to talk to Johnny and get him to talk back.

"Come on, Johnny. Say something!"

He gave his face a little slap, but there was no response. Billy then moved back and rested on his knees. Richard and Phoebus looked at one another and nodded.

"Billy," said Phoebus, "We never got to thank him for saving us from Valmont and the mistake we made working for him in the first place."

"Why the change of heart?" asked Billy.

"I saw something in Johnny I had not seen enter the Forest Region in a long time."

"Yeah? And what's that?" asked Billy.

"Determination."

"Doesn't everyone who enters trying to bring down Valmont have that?"

"Yes, but Johnny's was different. His determination was determination through love. The words he spoke. He didn't want to just kill Valmont to kill him and claim his title. He didn't care about any of that.

He wanted revenge on him for killing his father. I knew Valmont was a murderer, but those he killed were enemies to the land I call home."

"He was there for you when no one else was?" asked Billy.

"Essentially. On top of that, no one had ever come that close to killing me. Many skilled warriors have come in and have given me some bruises, sure, but none of them have ever been close to killing me. And in the end, I always won. Johnny knew he had me, but through his determination, he knew he wasn't going to kill me and just wanted me to cease fighting. That's how I regained the upper hand and was able to defeat him. I let him pass because of this . . ."

"Wow!" said Billy.

"Plus, the name Hunderson . . . I knew I had heard that name before. People had spoken a lot about a man who was going around the East End wreaking havoc and seeking answers. They did not however speak of why. When I saw Johnny and heard him speak of his reason, I knew it was he of whom the others spoke. It was then that my own will changed; my determination for protecting Valmont then became an immediate hatred. Valmont has protected me and these lands for many waves, but his way of protection is wrong," said Phoebus.

"What changed?" asked Billy.

"When we all first came here, he was very caring and also a bit paranoid, but we all saw past the paranoia and just saw the care. Over the waves he stopped caring for his sentries and just started caring that no one reached him. He started destroying nearby cities and villages. He killed innocent people. I didn't leave or try to stop him because I had no other purpose. No home to go to, no family to return to. Then, about six waves ago, he stopped. He hasn't left the

Forest Region since," said Phoebus.

"So he was the demon wreaking havoc all over? Our cousin was correct," said Billy.

"I don't know, but I do know Valmont said he was tired of hearing about his brother and his success, but he said he loved him nonetheless. I now know that the brother he speaks of is your father, John Hunderson Sr. When Johnny introduced himself, I knew I had heard the name 'Hunderson' before, but I just couldn't place it. I'm not saying your father is alive, but what I do know is that Valmont did not kill him. Nevertheless, Valmont also mentioned valuable information he had that people were seeking. This was the reason he had set up sentries."

"When I was picking up Johnny, I noticed Valmont had a tattoo of a Black Dragon's Foot on his upper right chest. I knew immediately I had some relation to him, but I did not know what," said Billy.

"He's your uncle, Billy," replied Phoebus.

"I only ever thought I had one uncle. My father never told me of any more family members. All I knew was my cousin Wallace. That and just my brothers. It makes me wonder if my father is still alive."

"Wallace, who is his father?" asked Richard.

"I don't know," said Billy.

"How did you not think you at least had another uncle or aunt?" asked Richard.

"I just said our father didn't tell us, but it did make us wonder when our brother Ryan asked us that we didn't find it curious that Wallace had a different last name than ours."

"He must have taken his mother's maiden name," said Richard.

"According to Valmont, your dad was last seen atop a clock tower in Wakesfield fighting this guy named Shadow."

"Who is he?" asked Billy.

"The Mystery Men leader," replied Richard.

"This is all so new to me. I've gone on adventures before, but never have I travelled so far away from home. I have a feeling I won't be seeing my home for a while now."

"No, Billy. You will be seeing your home. Return to your home. Forget any of this happened and just live your life," said Phoebus.

"How can you say that? First my father, then my brother Derex, and I can only assume Ryan, and now Johnny. Johnny was the closest family I had as the only other family I have is off in the war."

"And apparently back on the North End of the Forest Region," said Richard in a sarcastically dark tone.

"I said to return home, Billy, not to give up. You need to go home and train. Become stronger," said Phoebus.

"Valmont will come looking for you, so it's best you stay away for now," stated Richard.

"Why would he come looking for me?" asked Billy.

"It doesn't matter. Just stay safe. Return to your home and stay there," stated Richard.

"Well then, I guess that's it. We exchange stories then part ways, huh? Is that how far trust goes these days?" asked Billy.

"I'm sorry, Billy. I'll be heading to the Ice Region. I can only hope I'll find what I'm looking for there," said Phoebus.

"What if troubles rise? What then?" asked Billy.

"If trouble does come just know you have us as allies."

"*Us?*" asked Richard.

"Yes!" Phoebus said glaring at Richard, "Both of us."

"I have to go find someone who has wandered off. I don't know how much help I'd be anyway," said Richard.

"Who are you seeking?" asked Billy.

"None of your concern."

"Well, where is it you're going? Maybe we can be of help to one another. We're both seeking someone."

"I require no one's help," replied Richard in a stern voice.

"You'll help Johnny but not me?" asked Billy.

"My intention wasn't to help him. Phoebus was already there when I showed up so I . . ."

"So, you what?" said Billy rising, "You decided to act like a hero in hopes of killing him when no one was looking?"

"Unlike you two, I don't bear a hate for Valmont. I know who my father is; I have a family to return to."

Billy threw a punch at Richard and hit him in the face. Richard threw one back, but Billy dodged it. Phoebus stepped in.

"Both of you stop it right now! Can't you all tell there is something bigger going on than our quarrels? There is a war going on. Billy, if I weren't going to the Ice Region I would go with you, and where I go I cannot take you. I implore you to return to your home. Train. Get stronger. There is an approaching shadow and we all have to be ready for it. Now I don't know about Richard, but I know you have made an ally today. Here, take this."

Phoebus handed Billy a flare.

"A flare? Seriously? How are you supposed to see this if you're so far away? I looked at the map my brother left me. The Ice Region is leagues away from the Forest Region. At least thirty-day journey," Billy said as he spun the flare in his hand.

"This isn't any ordinary flare, Billy. Setting this off will trigger a chain reaction in the sky. Each flare that shoots off will eject another one, and another, reaching all the way to the icy sky above the Ice Region. Direfell is full of more than simply fighting. There are magical elements to it, as well," said Phoebus, with a grin.

"I'm to shoot the flare then simply wait one league for you to get to me?" asked Billy.

"There are other means of travel, faster ones. You should look more closely at that map of yours, Billy," said Phoebus.

"Just like through the Forest Region, right?"

"Exactly," said Phoebus.

"But nothing was on there . . ."

"Look more closely, all right? As far as this flare goes, this is as a last resort, you understand?"

Billy nodded.

"Just like those star letters Johnny saw," said Billy, quietly to himself, "I guess I'll make my way back to Wakesfield. I'll become stronger, and I'll avenge my brother's death!"

"Like I told your brother, Billy, revenge isn't always the best path on which to travel. However, with the determination from you Hundersons, I know that everything you do is with value and merit."

"What happens when we cross paths again," asked Billy.

"We won't," replied Richard, coldly.

"What is your problem, man?"

"My problem? It doesn't matter."

"You said you have no problem with Valmont and such, but clearly you have a problem because that man killed my brother. I can't even look at you."

"Then don't."

"My question just got answered. Richard, if you and I cross paths again, we're going to have a duel and you're going down."

"Why not settle this right now then," asked Richard, gripping his staffblade tightly.

Phoebus once again stepped in between their intense staring contest.

"Richard, don't be an idiot. Go off seeking what you must. If you don't want to befriend Billy, then I don't know what to tell you. You and I are best of friends, and I'm trusting Billy. I don't see why you can't, too," stated Phoebus.

Richard just stared at Phoebus.

"If this is really how we're parting, then I don't think I can accept this flare, Phoebus."

Billy extended out the flare to Phoebus.

"Keep it. You never know what the future will bring."

Richard scoffed.

"That goes for you, too, Richard," commented Phoebus.

Richard once again stared at Phoebus.

Phoebus turned and pulled out another flare. He knelt next to Johnny and tucked it under his arm, so it would be well hidden. He took out some sap and rubbed it on his wound, then nodded his head and rose back to his feet.

"Am I to just leave Johnny here?" asked Billy, staring at Johnny.

"It's best he remains here within the Forest Region to be allowed to heal," said Phoebus, pointing to the sap on his wounds.

"I don't want to lose him . . . He'll die here if the Elected Four comes out here."

"Billy, if you do decide to come back to the Forest Region and try to face Valmont, just be careful. I don't know what's going to happen now. Richard and I aren't returning so I imagine he'll replace us as sentries. Best of luck," said Phoebus, as he patted Billy on the shoulder.

"To you, too, Phoebus."

Billy knelt back down next to Johnny and he placed his hand over the Black Dragon's foot tattoo.

"I'm sorry I couldn't be there for you, but I *will* not let you down. I will return and avenge you," said Billy, rising back to his feet.

The last thing they all saw while they walked their separate ways out of the Forest Region was Johnny's body up against the tree, and as the sunlight broke through the trees, it shined its light right on him.

 *About the Author*

Michael J. Edwards (1994-) is a 27-year-old millennial born into the wrong generation. Delve into the mind of Michael as he creates and explores vivid, fantastical worlds. Michael began writing in the fifth grade with a pencil and a notebook, then moved onto Microsoft Word 1999 and floppy disks. Michael's passion for the written word continues as his writing evokes emotion and provides the reading world with new and fresh adventures.

www.ingramcontent.com/pod-product-compliance
Lightning Source LLC
Chambersburg PA
CBHW050416260626
47156CB00003B/1034